CW01637966

IN THE BEGINNING OF THE NIGHT

PETER RIMMER

ABOUT PETER RIMMER

Peter Rimmer was born in London, England, and grew up in the south of the city where he went to school. After the Second World War, aged eighteen, he joined the Royal Air Force, reaching the rank of Pilot Officer before he was nineteen. At the end of his National Service, he sailed for Africa to grow tobacco in what was then Rhodesia, now Zimbabwe.

The years went by and Peter found himself in Johannesburg where he established an insurance brokering company. Over 2% of the companies listed on the Johannesburg Stock Exchange were clients of Rimmer Associates. He opened branches in the United States of America, Australia and Hong Kong and travelled extensively between them.

Having lived a reclusive life on his beloved smallholding in Knysna, South Africa, for over 25 years, Peter passed away in July 2018. He has left an enormous legacy of unpublished work for his family to release over the coming years, and not only they but also his readers from around the world will sorely miss him. Peter Rimmer was 81 years old.

To read more about Peter's life, please visit his website: https://www.peterrimmer.com/novelist/author/

ALSO BY PETER RIMMER

The Brigandshaw Chronicles

The Rise and Fall of the Anglo Saxon Empire

Book 1 - Echoes from the Past

Book 2 - Elephant Walk

Book 3 - Mad Dogs and Englishmen

Book 4 - To the Manor Born

Book 5 - On the Brink of Tears

Book 6 - Treason If You Lose

Book 7 - Horns of Dilemma

Book 8 - Lady Come Home

Book 9 - The Best of Times

Book 10 - Full Circle

Book 11 - Leopards Never Change Their Spots

Book 12 - Look Before You Leap

Standalone Novels

All Our Yesterdays

Cry of the Fish Eagle

Just the Memory of Love

Vultures in the Wind

In the Beginning of the Night

The Asian Sagas

Book 1 - Bend with the Wind

Book 2 - Each to His Own

The Pioneers

Book 1 - Morgandale

Book 2 - Carregan's Catch

Novella

Second Beach

IN THE BEGINNING OF THE NIGHT

Copyright © Peter Rimmer 2021

This novel is entirely a work of fiction. Names, characters, long-standing establishments, places, events and incidents are either the products of the author's imagination or used in a fictitious manner. Any resemblance to actual persons, living or dead, is purely coincidental.

First published in Great Britain in December 2021 by

KAMBA PUBLISHING, United Kingdom

10 9 8 7 6 5 4 3 2 1

Peter Rimmer asserts the moral right to be identified as the author of this work.

All rights reserved. No part of this publication may be reproduced or transmitted in any form or by any means, electronic or mechanical, including photocopy, recording, or any information storage and retrieval system, without permission in writing from Kamba Publishing at books@peterrimmer.com.

FOREWORD

In the Beginning of the Night was a novel that my father, Peter Rimmer, began writing in 1966 and is thought to be one of his first pieces of work. It certainly is a departure, as far as we are aware, from most of his other novels, those being historical fiction, whereas this book is an adventure thriller. Peter was most assuredly honing his craft in his early years, so if you have read any of his later novels, like the *Brigandshaw Chronicles*, you will find the style of writing to be very different.

It is a story which will take you to a bygone era with places Peter definitely visited, most particularly the isle he and my mother, Rosemary, knew as Paradise Island in the Mozambique Channel. An island that was idyllic and adored by both. Sadly, it is no longer a tourist resort, but perhaps one day it may become so again.

We sincerely hope you enjoy this novel of adventure.

Heather Stretch
December 2021

1

SALISBURY, RHODESIA 1966

The "Fly CAA" sign had nothing but blue sky behind it. It looked down from the top of nineteen storeys on to a wide street of angle-parked cars that reflected the tropical sun. The street was wide enough to outspan two sets of oxen at the same time. The colours of summer dresses, and the people inside them, ignored this relevant fact as they dodged the streams of open-windowed cars going towards and away from the building that held up the Central African Airways sign. Below, the smaller, far less noticeable neon sign of Safaris (Pvt) Limited flashed a red strip around itself more in desperation than anything else. It was in hopeless competition with the glare of the sun.

The Safaris window display was a collection of travel brochures. Inside, Korina Prague looked, to the travel-hungry gazers on the wrong side of the plate-glass window, as if she enjoyed her job, although perhaps not as much as they enjoyed the sight of her. The two other girls among the spears and animal skins were almost as pretty. Around the walls were posters of lions that appeared half asleep but were full of eye-glint, elephants after mud baths and impala poised before flight from the click of a camera.

The movement of the young females was watched with interest by Herman Small as he waited to be served; he was able, he realised with particular satisfaction, to catch them from all angles as they moved from telephone to telephone. Korina Prague made him feel he was missing something, so he changed the weight of his body on to the other foot. The telephone nearest to him was a winner as she had to lean across the table towards him to pick it off the hook. It made him even more certain that his trip was going to be successful and that his father's money was not going to be wasted. He moved his weight back on to the other foot as she smiled at him while still talking into the telephone. He didn't listen to what she was saying. Her mouth was soft and full at the centre, the soft redness seemed to come out to him as she spoke. Her eyes were brown, large and compelling. She stood with her legs pressed against both sides of her green cotton skirt.

He could sense that other people were standing behind him but, with Korina Prague just two feet in front of him, he didn't have enough curiosity to turn round.

Finally, she put down the receiver and turned to them all.

"Ah... I can see you've all arrived. I'm Korina Prague. Mr Dacks will be off the telephone in a moment. Won't you all sit down. Welcome to Rhodesia."

He could hear a foreign accent in her voice, slightly guttural, but hidden, though he didn't know it, by the swallow-each-word technique of the Rhodesians. He continued to stare at her as she came around the desk; she ignored the renewed ringing of the telephones and walked into the centre of the group of passengers who had all been on Herman's flight. One, Anna Featherstone, was a girl even younger than himself with all her 'airs and graces' intact; a type he recognised and disliked. There were four others. His eyes went to a woman of thirty with heavy make-up, who flaunted both her poise and the rings on her fingers. There was a large emerald on the third finger of Francine Mure's left hand and, nearer the knuckle, a more reasonably sized solitaire diamond.

Korina Prague looked at the jewellery with appreciation and then smiled at the passengers in turn. Her message was felt by the men.

"I hope your flight from London was comfortable," she said. "The VC10 is usually very good… Ah, Mr Dacks is off the telephone. Will you follow me?"

Herman Small watched the tight movement of her rear as it went away from him towards the open door and passed into the glass-fronted office that looked out directly at the girls and the telephones and customers of the Safaris enterprise. His view was obscured by Mrs Hall, a well-corseted, short woman with dyed grey hair and expensive clothes. She walked with confidence to an easy chair, sat down and took the cigarette and light from Mark Dacks as if she had rehearsed the part for a stage-play.

Francine Mure caught Mark Dacks's eye and he wondered if the emerald was ever his; he smiled to himself, made his black eyebrows go up slightly and flicked the inside of his cheek with the tip of his tongue. She refused a First Lord cigarette from the copper cigarette box and immediately took a packet of menthol from her bag, ignoring his ignited lighter. He didn't offer Anna Featherstone a cigarette because he didn't believe in such things for one so young at the start of a tour.

The middle-aged Harold Ackit got in just before Herman Small; he was already smoking.

Herman made himself comfortable like the others, was grateful for the cigarette, and made a note not to inhale in front of so many people as the first drag usually turned him pale in the face and made his head fuzzy. His particular centre of interest, Korina Prague, stood behind the desk and leaned her thighs firmly against it; she wore neither jewellery nor rings.

The desk was clear of any papers. Two copper-bearing granite rocks, away from the clean blotting pad, were in one corner and a model meteor on a triangular stand was trying to take off from the other. A large, illustrated map of Rhodesia hung on the wall above Mark Dacks's head and the blue area of Lake Kariba was prominent. To the right was a glass-fronted cabinet complete with rock samples. Mauve crystals of amethyst stuck cleanly and unnaturally from a chunk of quartz. The cabinet was locked. One wall had a headless leopard-skin nailed to the wooden partition next to a small door that looked innocent but wasn't. The opposite wall, which would have led out on to the street wide enough to inspan oxen if it had had an opening, held up a framed picture of a low-level aerial photograph of Salisbury that showed off the skyscrapers to their best advantage. There was no wasted space in the room, which was just sufficient to seat five passengers.

Herman noticed Anna Featherstone's well-shaped, medium-long legs and was surprised that his eyes had strayed from desktop level and the central attraction of Korina Prague. He decided that maybe he'd begun to expect too much from the trip but continued to enjoy what he could see for the moment. He knew what he wanted and knew there was plenty of time.

Mark Dacks seated himself and imperceptibly brushed Korina Prague. Satisfied, he turned his attention to the watching, innocent passengers.

"Hello. I'm Mark Dacks and this is Korina Prague. Now, let me see if I can guess. Ah, you must be Mrs Hall."

"How clever of you to know."

Mrs Hall was in her sixties. She had fitted her cigarette into a stubby, workmanlike cigarette-holder and held it firmly from underneath, having taken it out of her mouth to speak. Her strong teeth clenched shut on the Bakelite again.

"And Mrs Cunningham."

"I used to be Mrs Cunningham but I'm now Mrs Mure."

"I'm sorry. And you are Miss Featherstone?"

"I think I'm the only girl left so you must be right."

"Now, you must be Mr Ackit and you Herman Small. Good, now we all know each other. A car is waiting to take you to Meikles Hotel where you will spend the first night. You'll have plenty of time to get some good sleep later and so be fit for the drive to Mana Pools tomorrow. No one enjoys anything if they are tired. The time is now nearly four o'clock, which will give you all time to change and be ready for a sundowner in my flat at six o'clock. You have paid a lot for this exclusive tour and though the friends who recommended it to you may have said it was worth every penny, we intend to prove it. Safaris never advertises. We rely on pleasing you, and on you and your friends coming back again. In the next six weeks we shall put five years of happy thoughts into your lives. This is a great country with everything to offer and I'll promise you now that you'll never forget it."

'And neither they will,' thought Korina, 'if they find out the true exclusiveness of the tour.' She then caught Herman Small gazing at the area just above her thighs and pressed them into the lid of the desk. She felt good.

Mark Dacks couldn't see any snags in the faces that looked at him. He took a cigarette for himself and considered that life was full of promise. He stood up to his full six feet, leaned his knuckles on the table and smiled at the room in general and then more particularly at the three women in turn. He decided that the younger one had promise. He also concluded, after looking at Francine Mure, that she must be an exceptional performer to have acquired so many rich husbands.

"The car will pick you up at six from the hotel. Dress how you like. We don't waste time out here making ourselves uncomfortable unless it is necessary. There'll be a buffet supper for those of you who'd like to stay. Make up your minds when you get there. It's always better to be spontaneous. You won't want to be back late at the hotel so this is why we're starting early. I hope you all enjoy Rhodesia, and look forward to seeing you this evening."

He came around the desk, treading firmly on the head of a badly cured leopard skin, pulled the door open and smiled them out towards the convertible Ford Galaxy that was waiting patiently beside the parking meter. He and Korina Prague exchanged glances as she followed the passengers towards the brilliant sunshine, then the smile faded from his face as the car slid away from the kerb and gave the CAA sign an interesting view of head-tops, dress-fronts and a sun-glinting bonnet. The exhaust fumes were lost in the moistureless brilliance of the highveld air.

2

SUNDOWNERS

"You look your most seductive in that outfit," commented Mark Dacks. "I hope that lad doesn't get too excited about the cleft in your dress or your curvy backside. Cultivate him, yes, but keep him under control."

"You make this sound like the first time, Mark." Korina Prague smiled at him.

"We must always think of it like that. It keeps the mind alert. They look a nice crowd and should enjoy themselves. I'll answer the doorbell. You keep standing there and stun them in your green dress. That colour is definitely yours. It would be nice to see you wearing one of the emeralds but that can't be helped."

Mark Dacks moved easily towards the front door of his penthouse. His white tuxedo, with the red band around a strong waist, matched the sun-drenched furniture in the throes of evening. The sun hit in across the roof garden in its last deluge and picked out the rich redness of the thick Persian carpets on the well-polished mukwa floor, overpowering the violent colours of a large abstract over the cocktail cabinet. The oiled wood of the front door glinted from its cracks. The French windows behind gave out into the pure, almost coolness of early evening air. The scent of jasmine was strong, sweet and exotic.

The door opened to his pull and Mrs Hall saw all of this in the flash of what would always stay in her memory. The sun bathed her harshly and picked out her age.

"I'm glad you got here first," said Mark Dacks. "It means we can have a quick drink before the others arrive. Please come in. You must have caught a taxi."

"No, I walked. I enjoyed myself. People were helpful and told me the way. The red flowering trees are quite lovely. I enjoyed the square with the fountain too. You have a beautiful city."

"I think so too, but then I'm biased. This is my country. What will you drink? How about a dry martini? In a week's time you'll want a longer drink but straight off the plane should see you along nicely with a cocktail. I make them specially myself."

"I always drink them at home. Hello, Miss Prague. You look very attractive in that dress. It suits you. This is all such a change from London. What a fantastic colour the sun is making out there in the sky as it sets. One has to get into the countryside in England to see the sunsets. Thank you, it looks just fine... Cheers... Yes, and it tastes good. May I go outside? I have never seen anything so lovely as that sunset. You have such a wonderful view from up here on top of so tall a building. No, you go and answer the bell. I am old enough to enjoy this by myself."

Mark Dacks looked out past her to the colours above the distant bush and around at the highveld clutching at Salisbury. The bush had allowed it only a small patch of the vastness of Africa. A jolt of pleasure kicked him in the stomach and reminded him that he was where he really wanted to be. The quick dusk had taken the colour out of the light away from the blazing smile of the setting sun. He turned round at the third buzz of the bell and strode towards the front door. He flicked on the light-switch as he trod the second carpet and the concealed lights spread a few inches up their pin-points of wall. It was the in-between of day and night. The sundowner. He opened the door to Anna Featherstone, Francine Mure, Harold Ackit and Herman Small. They filed in past his welcome to be greeted by the orange violence of the distant but dominant horizon. The drinks chinked and the laughter began.

The sun turned its back on the new night and drew with it the last colours from the bottom of the dome of sky. The fire of day was almost out.

Herman Small drank his beer with the usual pleasure and reminded himself of the warning he had been given about there being more alcohol in the beer than at home. He didn't mind making a fool of himself but he did dislike the hangovers. After filling his eyes to the full on Korina Prague's inviting cocktail poise, he slowly swivelled his eyes to Anna Featherstone. The expectant, frustrated surge rose in him sharply to a new high. He swallowed at the sight of soft, round breasts pushing firmly above the loose cut of an orange and black dress that flared from her waist and bust. Her bra was doing most of the job but he didn't care.

To counter his desire to touch her, he walked over to the cocktail cabinet and took another cold beer from the ice bucket as directed by Mark Dacks when he had been given the first. The new beer bottle frothed as promised. He poured into the side of his glass, put down the empty bottle and tasted the new beer with satisfaction. He wiped his mouth and took a First Lord from the packet newly offered to him by Mark Dacks and decided he liked the man. He tried to hold himself a little straighter as a result.

As Dacks offered to get Mrs Mure another drink, Herman thought he would offer his services to Anna Featherstone.

"I thought you were one of those rugby types who stand in groups of men if they can find them, or by themselves if they can't, and drink beer," she said in answer to his offer. "Yes, I'd love another sherry out of the dark bottle. I know it's wrong to admit it, but I like sherry sweet."

She leaned slightly forward and finger-tapped the cork of the bottle in question. He took hold of the bottle, uncorked it and poured into her glass, taking advantage of the opportunity to take in another two inches of her cleavage. As he looked up, he realised that Korina Prague had seen where he had been looking. He involuntarily gave her half a wink and got an even smaller one back.

"I gave up playing sport at school," he told Anna, "and though it may not be long ago, it seems to me like a lifetime. I don't have the time."

As he spoke, he studied the girl more carefully. Her skin was not perfect but its imperfections were covered by make-up. The eyes had a depth that he hadn't seen before, although that could be the second beer talking. Her brown hair was half-way to her shoulders and returned a glint of gold as she moved. Her shoulders were smooth and crossed by a thin white strap on either side.

"What do you do instead?" Anna asked him.

"Nothing really, but I still don't have the time. It's too difficult to train and keep fit in the suburbs. You look daft running around the houses in a natty pair of white shorts, and it's too damned hot after half a mile in a tracksuit. I spend three hours travelling to and from the office every day, so there we have it."

"How did you get away for this trip?"

"I resigned. Life's too short not to do so. Two weeks by the sea each year for fifty years is not what I want. Father agrees, and as he has plenty of money he doesn't mind paying the bill. He hopes I may fall in love with a country like this and stay here. He's sick of my moans about England. I enjoy it at times, sure, but mostly it gives me claustrophobia. Probably something to do with the smog. It's getting worse in the City and this year it went all yellow in the street lights. Not the atmosphere to thrive in. Maybe it's just me. I haven't found what I want to do so I just keep travelling along like Old Man River."

"It sounds rather boring not to have an aim in life."

"Let me top up that sherry for you. Nothing is more boring than a sober party. I have a feeling that Mrs Hall drinks. I've seen her have three of his special martinis and she hasn't turned a hair, and I'm sure she's meant to. I saw him mix the second lot and the amount of Vermouth he put in wasn't even worth a smell. I think you're safer on the sherry. How did they let you come on a trip like this by yourself?"

"I'm nineteen, you know. Mummy says that if I can't look after myself at this age, I never will. And I can, too. I don't like fast men, or men to touch me at all, in fact."

Uncomfortably, he moved those three inches away from her and got back to propriety.

"But you dress to kill them none the less."

"Oh, no, I never thought of it like that. It's just fashion that dictates what I wear, and if fashion says this then I can't disagree with it. I mean, I'm just one among so many."

"What made you choose a holiday in Africa?"

"None of my friends have been here. They all know Majorca, Bermuda and the Greek islands like they do Piccadilly Circus but they haven't heard of Mana Pools."

"I presume your father paid for your trip as well."

"Oh, but who else?"

"I thought Mr Ackit over there might be willing to help."

"I think that's vulgar."

"I'm pulling your leg, Anna Featherstone, pulling your leg."

"I'm sorry. I didn't think of it as a joke."

"Mine are never very good. All that can be said for them is that I try. Do you mind if I help myself to another beer? I rather like this Lion ale. They find the most original names for their beers. After this next one I'll turn over to the Cinzano. I'm beginning to feel the altitude and the alcohol already."

"Do you mean you're getting drunk?"

"No, not that, but it is enabling me to find everyone more attractive."

"I'll take that as a compliment and go and talk to Miss Prague."

"In that case I'll follow you as I too would like to talk to Miss Prague."

"I'M glad the young couple have found something to talk about," Mark Dacks was meanwhile telling Harold Ackit. "They seem to be getting along well. It's luck when the ages fit on our tours, Mr Ackit."

"Try Harold, it's easier. If I were younger I'd appreciate his luck, though I'd put my money on his eye being more on your Miss Prague. I think I'd have had my eye on her myself twenty years ago. I expect she allows life to take her where she wants to go and that's how it should be. Have you always been in the travel business?"

"For eight years. Yes, it's interesting. There are always new places to discover for people. It will be the first time we've taken a tour to Mana Pools. I'm sure you'll find it the game country you thought couldn't really exist."

"What were you doing eight years ago?"

"Enjoying myself too much most of the time."

"But always in Rhodesia?"

"Shall we say mostly in Africa. My grandfather came up on a wagon from Beira in 1896 and ever since then the Dacks family have been addicted to Africa. We've tried our hand at many things and enjoyed most of them, which is all of the battle really. Can I give you another Scotch? The ice hasn't melted yet. Have you ever thought of investing money in Africa?"

"I've thought of investing money in most places but not very often in Africa. The only time I tried was with de Courcy's New Cerny and that white elephant of a township can be seen about twelve miles from here in amongst the weeds and crumbling bricks."

"That wasn't a good example of investment potential, as Mr de Courcy found out to his cost when he went to jail. Other men have made honest thousands. How is taxation in England?"

"Appalling."

"Now you see my point, but I'm sure you don't want to think about money on your holiday. Come across and I'll introduce you to Mrs Mure. I'm sure you'll find something in common. Mrs Hall, come across and join us. That sky has gone forever, I'm afraid."

"Quite magnificent. I'll have another drink if I may."

"There's plenty made... How's that?"

"Fine."

"Have you met Mr Ackit?"

"Not properly. So how do you do."

"And Mrs Mure. Mrs Hall and Mr Harold Ackit."

"Hello. I seem to have heard that name Ackit before."

"Probably in connection with banking, Mrs Mure. Mr Ackit is a partner in the firm of Cornell and Ackit, Commercial Bankers of Lombard Street."

"You know all the facts, Mark."

"You forget I know Percy Cornell, but, even then, it is my job to know these things."

'You can say that again,' thought Korina without turning towards him or giving her two young admirers the slightest idea that she was listening to more than their conversation. There had been a time when she was interested in very young men and could get some satisfaction out of showing them more than even their youthful little minds could conjure. But not anymore.

The wall lights took control from the dying sunset, to the relief of Francine Mure, who knew she looked better in softer light. In Mark Dacks she saw a little of the old feeling in what had become her tired sex-life. She was pleased there was something left and had an urge to stroke his well-made neck. Provided there was something of definite interest just ahead for her she ignored the longer future and put back the fear of endless boredom into its proper place. The spark of ignition pulled her again as she looked deep into his eyes. He smiled with a friendly pleasure which her long experience told her they understood each other and that all good things could be had in the future.

Harold Ackit recognised the symptoms of divorce in Mrs Mure and felt the nag of his private life returning. It was like any good migraine. He had hoped, among other things, that by going so far from England, the nagging dissatisfaction would be left behind, but here it was again. His partner had done the trip the previous year with a girlfriend. Harold Ackit had now come to see for himself. At the moment he saw nothing powerful behind the white tuxedo, but then he was prepared, which was something.

He found himself speculating on the financial success of Dacks's tours. It puzzled him to find only four paying companions even though he had paid a little over a thousand pounds for his ticket, which included free drink and everything. He couldn't see Dacks fitting in more than four trips a year to be outside the rains when a number of the more interesting places would become inaccessible. Twenty thousand gross, therefore, from which airfares, food, hotel bills et cetera all had to be paid, together with the pleasure of his and the girl's company! It didn't look a lot to Harold Ackit, and it added an element of certainty to the already certain convictions of his partner.

"Will you have another drink, Harold? You look way off in your own thoughts. Don't worry about what you've left behind. It's not worth it."

An African waiter carried in a saddle of cold beef and placed it on the sideboard beside a long-bladed, bone-handled knife. Harold Ackit's glass clinked against the refilling bottle. The kitchen door opened again and the same waiter brought in an oval dish of cold, tin-foil-roasted guinea fowl. The salads and fruits followed. The pale green lettuce blended with the well-roasted beef and the yellow of the pineapple. The gamebirds crouched beside spring onions and radishes and the open halves of green avocado, whose insides had been mushed up with salt, pepper and vinegar.

"Everything we eat or drink here was grown in Rhodesia. We think our beef is the best in the world and hope you'll agree. To get the right taste it has to be cooked in a large piece. You'll see what I mean when I cut it open. There, the meat is red consistently and yet it doesn't run blood, and because it has been cooked on the bone it will taste all the better. Come around and tell me how much you'd like. The avocado is an acquired taste, but when you've got it there's nothing better."

Mrs Hall viewed the food with satisfaction and looked forward to the coming eight weeks of such fare with relish. She regarded her immediate life as a success that would continue, so long as her health remained to enjoy so much food and drink and new places; people too. She had stopped worrying about where she was coming from or going to on her fifty-third birthday. She had produced four children, loved her deceased husband as much as anything in her life and had concluded that all that was past was finished and that the future was hers to be used as she wished. She believed that selfishness was an inherent source of pleasure, and provided the self-interest didn't inflict harm on others, it could only create good for her. She took a spoonful of the avocado and put it in her mouth, then another and another. She moved her tongue tentatively over her palate.

"I wish I had acquired this taste earlier. These are magnificently piquant after the Gin and French. I can see you like food as well as your wine, Mr Dacks. Yes, I think I can eat another slice of beef. It looks as good as anything I had with Thomas before the war. He would have enjoyed this trip and I only hope he can see me wherever he is, as I'm sure he'd want me to enjoy myself. I only spend the interest on what he left me and never the capital, so I don't feel bad. Mind you, I could spend it all if I wanted to, but he trusted me and knew I wouldn't. That is why he left it all fluid."

She spooned another helping of avocado into her mouth with satisfaction and accepted with a nod the frosted glass of red wine that was put on top of the radiogram for her by Korina Prague. Her smile mingled with impulsive alarm at being served a red wine that was not at room temperature. She decided the Rhodesians were very good but not fully informed in the correct ways. She would mention it to Mr Dacks at a more suitable moment.

The group had begun to grow accustomed to one another. The thoughts in four of the passengers' minds were on new pleasures and places. The thoughts of one were private. The thoughts of two were on meeting places in the bush, and the chains of confidence throughout the Congo, Zambia, Malawi, and Mozambique, and Rhodesia that fruitfully culminated in the hands and bank balance of Mark Dacks. The five new arrivals were to fit into the next chain of confidence; their predecessors in the last eight years had been totally unaware of their parts and had therefore played them beautifully. One of their cases had gone astray at Victoria Station but so far it hadn't turned up in the wrong hands. The insurance company had paid for the case and clothes therein some three years before.

Mark Dacks didn't need the bank or the money; it was the game that was important to him. He was a man of passion, one who could only survive in the modern world if he did so in the space and harshness of the African highveld. He was like his father and grandfather in that regard, but for them their fight for survival had been sufficient excitement; the game had almost ended for his grandfather in the Matabele Rebellion of 1896. In the much-changed Africa of his own generation, Mark Dacks had found it necessary to find something to do with his peculiar talents, but the 'something' had not been available in the normal avenues of progress. So he had decided to make up his own.

3

MANA POOLS

The lizard climbed diagonally up the window-gauze a foot above the headboard and two feet above the wide-open eyes of Herman Small. The coughs, grunts, shrieks and occasional trumpeting seemed to be in bed with him. He had been awake for several hours but the night was still in its prime. He had sweated and his pillow was soggy. To take his mind off the spine-chilling bush noises from just outside the flimsy structure built on wooden stilts and called a tree-top hotel, and to prevent himself imagining an elephant scratching its back successfully on the underside of the half-inch boarding that separated him from the wilds, he thought of Anna Featherstone, found little joy yet again and once more turned his thoughts to the more certain satisfaction derived from picturing Korina Prague. A hippo, though Herman Small didn't know what it was, ploughed its way back into the river some two hundred yards away and created, unwittingly, a little more sweat on Herman Small's pillow. There was no moon. Only a complete darkness. The noises were magnified many times over by the greater silence and the tension continued to rise in his belly.

OUTSIDE, Korina Prague moved silently away from the heavy mass that made up the 'hotel' and, with the .375 held as tightly as its weight would allow, worked her way between the shapes of trees and bushes towards the smell of the river. The hunting lamp was strapped to her head and the switch and battery bumped unsuspectingly against the skin-tight trousers over her left thigh. There was no sweat from her fear. She methodically searched for movement with her eyes, ears and nose and suppressed the powerful tension that gripped her body. She had done it many times before but the tension never diminished.

Mark Dacks once noted that, besides her intense determination, her success was probably due to this ability to control her fear. She wished now that Mark Dacks was with her, but knew that the danger could appear just as easily at the hotel. She stopped to listen, gave each noise the name of an animal or bird and moved on. The river sounded gentle and cool. The trees were silent. The light of stars barely penetrated the lacework above her. She went on and the dull sheen of the big river appeared through the trees. The trees passed on either side and her feet sank into the beginnings of sand. The last branches leaned over the sand towards the river. The river dominated. She went to within ten feet of the water and waited. Methodically her eyes searched the river, the Rhodesian shore to right and left, and, more thoroughly, the other side in Zambia. She saw nothing unnatural and, being out in the open with more time to use her gun, allowed some of the tension in her to relax. Sometimes she had waited for two hours and gone back empty-handed before the dawn and the guests woke up. She switched on the hunting lamp briefly twice and continued to look across at Zambia. The police, watching for saboteurs coming across the border, had made their job more difficult. She and Mark Dacks could tell them a thing or two about saboteurs and even more about the feelings in the two territories, but that would not be to their advantage.

She had learnt from him three years before that his family had lived in that part of Africa since the latter part of the nineteenth century. His old grandfather, in later years a native commissioner after one of his friends had talked him into passing on some of his knowledge of the country and people to younger men, had administered an area that stretched right up the valley on both sides of the river. That was before the Colonial Office in London had made a strict line of the border. The Dacks family, father, son and grandson, had spoken the tribe's language for seventy years.

Even in modern times, Mark Dacks had more influence over the five thousand square miles than the two governments, black and white respectively. With Korina's help, he used this influence to the benefit of them all, as well as the benefit of the distant friends of the tribe, who had trekked over the previous hundred years into the lower Congo, and to the east right through to the Mozambique coast. His sphere of authority was wide but little known to Europeans.

"What's the point of boasting?" he had once said to Korina when she'd asked him why he kept it so secret. She still remembered the gleam of intrigue in his eyes. In his father's day the matter was known to everyone, including the people in London, but later they operated at night and went under cover of fitfully sleeping guests in adjacent camps and hotels. The name Dacks fell out of official reports. Or so he hoped.

She enjoyed her rendezvous more afterwards than at the time of waiting. They made her more vital and alive to the touches of subsequent pleasure. Her sense of taste, sleep and wakefulness became stronger. Her enjoyment of life did not degenerate. There could be no complacency as there would soon be another time that would perhaps not be successful.

"Are you looking for me, *Enkorsikas*?" The tension in her ripped up to its maximum. She forced herself to release her caught breath.

"No, I'm not looking for anyone. And you, who are you seeking?"

She turned slowly and made herself smile to show whoever it was the whites of her teeth. An African was standing motionlessly in front of the trees at the top of the river bank. She wondered how long he had been there and whether he had seen her flashing her torch. There had been no reply from the other side. She decided to say that she was testing the battery. She had realised who he was by the fact that he spoke perfect English in a place so far from civilisation.

"It's a beautiful river, isn't it?" she said. "I would like to be able to afford to come here more often but Salisbury is a long way away and we only conduct a safari four times a year."

"You are with the party at the new tree-tops. It is a good hotel?"

"Yes, the tourists like it, I think. This is our first trip here."

"Do you know how to use that gun?" he said. He walked towards her down the sand. He was dressed in old shorts and a shirt of many holes. There were no shoes on his feet. She stopped herself taking a step backwards.

"Not really, but it gives me a safer feeling. I hadn't seen the river at night before and wanted to badly."

"It is very late in the night and dark."

"It is very hot and sleep is bad. And you, do you live in the valley? I must be nearer my home than you."

"I have a tent in the bushes half a mile up the river. There are two of us."

"And what do the two of you do in so remote a part?"

"Watch the river... And people... I'm sorry I frightened you. You must find it strange talking to me in English when I'm dressed like this but it is my new uniform. We play little games with the people who want to come across from the other side without their passports. It is easy to come in the right way so anyone coming across here must have something to hide."

"You must be special branch police."

"Yes, madam. I am Sergeant Mzingwa. We are placed at intervals all the way up the river but even then it is a big river to guard."

"You did frighten me, but I knew who you were when you spoke such good English. It is nice to know that people as good as you are watching our borders. Have you caught anyone yet?"

"No, but I may have stopped a number coming across, which is very good in itself."

"I must go back to the hotel. I shall sleep better knowing you are here. I like the police, and especially the BSAP. Goodnight."

"Goodnight, *Enkorsikas*. I hope I don't hear of you using that lamp, as I think in regulations it says they are illegal."

"I believe they are, but self-preservation, I think, comes before regulations."

She walked towards the trees. A moment later she felt happier in the deep shadows than she had done before. Her mind ignored the bush noises. She was annoyed and knew that Mark Dacks would be too. But she told herself that she was not to have known that there would be a plain-clothes policeman hiding in the bush just where she wanted to be on her own. 'Unless they know something and he was watching me!' she thought. No, that couldn't be. For one thing they'd never used this spot before and always made contact at Kariba or the Falls. Even there, they'd been coming and going with tourists to make their frequent visits seem natural. No, she told herself. Sergeant Mzingwa was looking for political criminals and was bored with his lot and wanted someone to talk to. His job must be lonely.

She saw the hotel more clearly through the trees as her eyes were used to the dark. She stopped short and watched, then moved forward to the wooden stairs and climbed up to the height of the poles and the entrance. She went in and down the passage to the bottom door on the left and opened it without knocking and went inside. Mark Dacks had his back to her. He was looking out of the window at the night.

"Did you get them?" He didn't turn round.

He had heard her easily, despite her stealth.

"No, there was a damn policeman acting as immigration personified. He saw me a long time before I saw him. He's had more practice."

"Blast."

"I thought more than that. I don't think he saw me use the lamp, and if he did he thought it of no consequence. There was no answer from the other side."

"I hope they didn't see you. I'd hate them to come across looking for us and bump into your friend. They'd get picked up on more than one account."

He turned around and began gathering his things to leave.

"Where are you going?" she asked.

"To Zambia. I'm going to stop them coming across now we have company."

"What are you going to use… A fast launch?"

"No, Korina, I'm going to swim. I know every current in this river. It won't take me more than ten minutes to get across."

"That's if the crocs let you pass."

"It's too dark for me to see them and vice versa. Anyway, it wouldn't be the first croc to get itself killed by a Dacks's knife. Kiss me and I'll go. Thanks for extracting yourself from the police force. Mmm, you taste good. If I'm not back by dawn, think up a story for our guests. I'll have to wait until the moon has gone. We'd intended on them staying here for two days, and you're a very good hostess. They look an easy lot to handle."

"Be careful, Mark."

He opened the door silently, looked out, then went quickly. The door closed soundlessly behind him.

As the dawn made its first, violently red impressions on the last of the night, Korina woke with a male hand gently stroking her belly-button. The face just above hers was dripping water onto her chin. The man was naked except for a belt with a long hunting knife attached on one side and a small canvas pouch hanging from the other – the jockey underpants were as wet as his hair and did very little for his morality. She pulled his head down to hers and kissed him before he picked her out of the bed and carried her to the window.

"How's that for a sunrise? This is the most beautiful country in the world. I hate to say this but you'll have to get back to your room. I don't want any of our friends thinking badly of us."

"I see you got the pouch."

"Yes, and a crocodile. I swam into the bastard and woke him up. We were surprised to see each other. Being fully awake, I had time to rip his belly open first. I'd have liked to have kept the skin but there were other matters on my mind, especially his relatives, who like the smell of blood, and our watcher on this side. He may have seen the scuffle, but to him it could have been anything. Anyway, he didn't blow his whistle."

"One of these days your luck may run out. It makes me afraid for you. Hand me my trousers. I may meet someone in the corridor."

She dressed in two strangled movements, walked to the door, looked around it and slid through the gap. Dacks shut it behind her.

There was just enough light for her to see down the corridor. She did up the last button of her shirt as Herman Small came out of his room hoping that the faint glimmer of light had made it safe enough for him to relieve himself in the lavatory across the way.

"Couldn't sleep, couldn't sleep. Were you the same?" he said.

"No, I slept well. I always get up with the dawn. It's the best time of the day. Why don't you put on some day clothes so I can show you the river?"

"Will we be safe?"

"Oh yes. All the animals are tame."

"I think you're pulling my leg, but I'll come just the same. I think I'd better go into the bathroom first for a wash. Give me three minutes."

She walked to her own room, opened the door and went inside. She walked across to the far side and picked up the face flannel from her dressing table, dipped it in the water tumbler and cleaned her face. She put on lipstick and a little blue eye-shadow and black eye-liner with smooth, accurate strokes. She knew she would look her best by the time the African sun rose a little higher.

She opened her suitcase and took out a powder-blue band for

her hair and pushed it into place. She was not pleased at having to prove her proclaimed habit of getting up early but she accepted it with good grace, patted down her shirt, blinked her eyes hard at the newly appeared treetops and sun outside the wooden-framed windows and walked over and opened the door and looked straight into the face of a frightened Herman Small. She decided that he must have had a worse night than she imagined and instinctively took his hand to reassure him that the world was friendly.

"We may see some game. When they put in the salt lick the game will come right up to the hotel! Have you ever seen big game before?"

"Only in the zoo. Are you sure it's safe to walk into the cage?"

"It's been done before. Now how does the dawn look with the door open? Quick… Over there… See it… It's a warthog. A large type of pig. Those tusks are as sharp as razorblades. Now he's frightened and runs away."

"He may hide and wait for us. Don't you think we should go back? I mean I'm not a coward but sense is sense and if those tusks are as sharp as you say."

"He's far more frightened of us than we are of him. He'll be a long way away by now and still running. Come on, let's go."

The new light picked out the trees in detail. Further on, they could see the river. They walked quickly through the trees along a game path. There was no sign of the policeman nor the dead crocodile, which was most likely being digested in the bellies of half a dozen of its closest relations. The Zambian shore was barren of life or sound. A fish eagle dived at the water and miraculously pulled up sharply with a baby bream in its beak. Korina pointed out to Herman all she could and her memories of the night seeped out into the crystal morning.

As they walked on, Herman felt his confidence returning and with it his appreciation of Korina. He decided he would like to pat her bottom but restrained himself. She was very nice to him. They walked to the river's edge and watched the ebb and flow and purity of the water. The water lapped at his sandalled feet and darkened a patch of the leather on each. He raised his eyes and let them travel out along the water and on into Zambia and up the white sand into the bush.

Meanwhile, Korina's eyes travelled away to her left, along the Rhodesian shore and then carefully along the line of bush that flanked the dunes. A small, palm-like tree leaned out of the sand at the point her eyes stopped. She looked more carefully and the human figure was transformed back into a tree stump.

Some thirty yards deeper into the bush, a pair of watching field-glasses were shielded from the glint of the sun. They walked up the river and the field-glasses were discarded as unnecessary. The irises of one pair of eyes were steel blue and the hair above was quite blond. The night-glasses that had unsuccessfully tried to make sense of the argument in mid-stream at three o'clock that morning were in their case at his feet.

"More bloody tourists." The blue eyes grew colder.

"She was the one last night."

"Doesn't look the type to smuggle in troublemakers. She looks all woman and nothing else. Let's go. You were right, there isn't anything to report about this lot. In a few years' time there won't be anywhere worthwhile to live that isn't swarming with people."

He spat quietly into the dry bush to further his point. The African sergeant followed suit to emphasise his full agreement. Silently, the European constable and Sergeant Mzingwa moved deeper into the bush, stopping as they unexpectedly flushed a water buck.

Korina Prague's eyes flashed to the movement.

"Look at that," she said. "A water buck. Isn't he beautiful as he jumps?"

The buck crashed out of sight. The policemen waited and moved on, bent double, out of sight.

A smile seeped into the brown eyes on the Zambian side that had seen, even at such a distance, the reason for the buck running. The African was sure now, that any danger was over and that Mark Dacks had reached the other side of the river safely. The brown eyes looked at the river and fear came into them at the thought of swimming so much water with the hippo and the croc. He again inspected his expertly camouflaged dugout, then, satisfied, started the long walk back to his kraal with the kraal's new money inside the handle of his knobkerrie.

"It is a safer way of getting food," he told himself, "rather than chancing with the rains."

He tried to calculate how many cattle could be bought from what was inside his knobkerrie and saw in his mind's eye a large group of long-horned cows and bulls. They would have added up to over two hundred head if he had been able to count. He was well satisfied with the thought of so many cattle, if a little puzzled at how easily the little white stones could be turned into the status symbol of his tribe. He concluded to himself that the people of the kraal would have to find more of these stones for next year. He thought of the policemen again and chuckled drily to himself.

THE THREE WOMEN on the tour had not yet come down from their bedrooms. Harold Ackit, coming back from his own private look at the bush, was pleased to smell his breakfast and to see it cooking on an open fire just outside the thatched hut ten yards from the main building he had slept in. The bacon, especially, produced a flood of saliva along his taste buds. The breakfast table was set out on trestles just in front of the heavy, white-ant-treated poles that held up the bedrooms.

Mark Dacks was watching two Africans lay out the cutlery, cups and tin side-plates on the long table. He thought briefly of a successful night. He had enjoyed for some years outwitting the monopolists and putting a good income into the kraals. Even more, he had enjoyed the danger. He smiled at Harold Ackit but looked nothing like the swimmer of four hours previously. They wished each other a good morning, which it was for both of them.

Korina and Herman came in from their walk and were drawn to the waiting table and long benches.

The young girl, Anna Featherstone, came down the wooden stairs from the bedrooms in a white two-piece arrangement that clearly showed everyone her firm, perfectly round navel. Herman Small remembered, on seeing this and experiencing a strange feeling in the pit of his stomach, that this was also the fashion in London. He congratulated himself on being so lucky with the season. He liked, very much, the tight shape of Anna's navel and would willingly have put his little finger as far inside as he could make it go. She trilled a good morning and spoiled the effect for him. He hoped that with a little familiarity he would grow used to her voice.

The fifty-yard clearing among the tall mopane trees had been cleared of elephant grass and roughly levelled. Rays of sun filtered through the forest of surrounding trees and patterned the table and waiting people. The powerful heat of day was growing with the sun's ascent. Birds of the richest colours called to themselves from the heights of the sprawling branches. There were the lime-green wings and lilac and blue breasts of the pigeons, and Mark Dacks even thought the bird at the top of the tree nearest to him had the glint of crimson. This, he decided, was taking things too far, so he returned his focus to organising the food. He considered the idea of a beer before breakfast, glanced up to see Mrs Hall coming down the wooden steps with forced precision and discarded the thought.

Francine Mure saw from beneath the weight of her mascara that Mark Dacks was wearing immaculately laundered white shorts and a white shirt that displayed the potential power in his shoulders. Again she remembered what she had missed during the night. It had taken her a long time to repair her face well enough to see the sun, which was why she was the last down to breakfast. She was wearing flesh-coloured tights and a knotted-in-front pink shirt. She hoped this might do the trick. The weight of her hair was pushed to one side.

Mark Dacks thought she looked twenty-five on the stairs but lost this illusion when she reached the trestle table and caught the full glare of a sunbeam in her face.

The food was brought to the table on four long platters, which were placed in front of Korina along with a pile of aluminium plates for distribution. Eggs, bacon, sausages, kidneys and fried green peppers were heaped on the platters and went off down the table, watched by the unfed guests. A waiter poured the tea for each guest. Mark Dacks watched him fill his own cup, then floated two thick slices of lemon into the black steaming liquid, added one small spoonful of Rhodesian sugar and stirred, the exercise taking his full concentration. Satisfied, he put the spoon in the saucer, gently lifted the heavy cup, blew the lemon slices expertly to the far side of the cup and drank in a slurp of the hot liquid. He looked back down the line of his guests and smiled before speaking.

"It's a good idea, Anna, trying for a suntan first thing in the morning, but by nine o'clock you must wear a hat and cover up. People from England get sunstroke very quickly out here and that wouldn't do for your holiday. There'll be plenty of sun, so take it in easy stages! It's all right, ladies and gentlemen, that was indeed the roar of a lion, but some half a mile away. He's telling his mate about a kill and calling her up for some breakfast. Now, who wants some more toast? Yes, I think a dozen slices are needed, Dinga, to start with."

Mark Dacks began with expert precision on his breakfast and the proceeds of good cooking rapidly began to disappear from his plate. He slightly raised his fork to address them again.

"We will show you plenty of game at Mana Pools before we move on into Zambia and back to comparative civilization at the new Casino Hotel beside the Victoria Falls. This, all around us, and in particular down there through the trees to the river, is the real Africa and the one that will be spoilt last. Herman and Anna will tell their grandchildren about the last tracts of Africa they saw as virgin bush but they won't be believed, because all this, by then, will only be a memory, a piece of history. Oh, and I didn't imply that the grandchildren would have one set of grandparents, though stranger things have happened on the Dacks Tours."

Korina agreed with his last sentiment, but didn't look up.

4

SECRET ASSIGNATIONS

Mark Dacks watched the mixing of his gin sling with care. The fresh lime juice, half a tot, followed the double tot of English gin into the tall, fluted glass. Ice-cold soda water topped up the glass and was joined by a half slice of lime before the whole was briskly stirred. The barman passed the full glass expertly across the new Safaris bar.

Mark gently raised the glass and brought it up to his mouth without shaking a drop from the brim. He drank slowly and without thirst and imperceptibly raised his right, dark eyebrow as he drank past the '1 a.m.' handwritten by a diamond on the inside of the glass. The letters only showed when the liquid tilted, entered the grooves and reflected the neon lights of the bar into his eyes. He drank a little more and the letters D G appeared below the time. He glanced amiably around the half-empty bar to check that no one was watching, then drained the glass.

As he reached the heavy glass doors of the bar that held in the air-conditioning, he heard the crunch of glass, a result of too vigorous polishing, and smiled to himself. He pulled the door handle towards him as directed by the sign at eye-level and was just in time to greet Mrs Hall on her way to the day's first dry martini. Dacks winced, remembering how much lager she had drunk with her curry at lunchtime, then changed his expression to a smile.

"Have you time for a small drink with me, Mr Dacks?" she asked.

"I only had time for a quick one just now. Later, though, I'd enjoy one with you. The barman will mix you the perfect dry martini if you tell him you like them like mine. They were very lucky to attract him across from the old hotel. They must pay him some very good money."

"I'll look forward to seeing you later."

The warm, humid air that then greeted him considerably reduced his ease of breathing.

As he reached the main stairs that led up to his bedroom wing, his forehead was wet with perspiration. A solid globule of sweat dribbled over the lobe of his right ear and dropped off onto the cream linen of his tropical suit. His black eyebrows lifted in a touch of displeasure.

As he moved his way up the circular stairs he checked on the reception area of the hotel below. It was their second evening in the hotel but he still checked carefully to be sure that Korina's brush with the BSAP at Mana Pools had been just a coincidence. He had seen no one to arouse his suspicion but this didn't reduce his concern. Eight clean years were not to be lost by momentary carelessness.

Reaching the top of the stairs, he turned right and walked briskly along a central corridor with the bedroom suites on either side. As usual, he had the room at the far end on the left. His guests flanked him and kept at a distance anyone he didn't know or hadn't been able to check up on. Korina was opposite, across the red strip of carpet from his room. He waited a moment in silence and then opened this door and quickly went inside. He was too quick for the moving sheet that streaked to cover her naked body. He noticed with pleasure the rich tan of her skin in contrast to the pure white pattern left by her bikini.

"Don't you ever wear any clothes?"

"The air-conditioning hasn't had a chance to clean out the humidity. I was beginning to enjoy its new coolness until you burst in. There's no privacy in this world with Mark Dacks around. Come and sit down on the bed."

"One a.m. at Devil's Gorge. I'm going to go myself. If the police think they've found out who's doing it, they may be waiting to catch one of us with the stones and if that's the case they're going to be suspicious of me and not you. I'm going to stay up drinking late and then persuade Francine Mure to come for a walk in the moonlight to look at the Falls. It's a regular thing in these parts and should be the perfect cover, especially if she's had a few drinks herself."

"I don't like you out late with that woman. She's too experienced."

"Business is business. Will you ask them to serve dinner for our party at eight? We'll have it in the room next to the tables. I like to watch rich people losing money; they're often so sharp at business and so foolish at the tables. The sun's almost gone. It's making rich colours of the 'smoke that thunders'. I'm off for a nap. How are you getting along with junior?"

"He's rather sweet, but I think he'll eventually go after the girl. Harold Ackit has forgotten his age and his family. He's got something, money, so just you watch our Mrs Mure."

"All right."

Dacks moved to her and quickly bent his head to hers to kiss her and just as quickly moved back to the door, opened it and went outside.

Korina slowly edged the sheet off her body and showed all of herself to the whispering touch of the newly cool air that circulated around her bed and the lower levels of the room.

'It's a pity he didn't have time for more,' she thought to herself.

She took her naked self off the bed and walked to the airtight window to confirm that the last red gush of the sun was behind the mountains of spray flung back by the impact of fallen water on the hard rock of the gorge. She, 'the smoke that thunders' and the red sun were each naked and transfixed in their own separate ways. She ran the palm of her right hand over her stomach. The firmness satisfied her. She had never had to diet.

She went over to the cupboard, unlatched the oak-fronted door and swung it open. She rummaged inside until her right hand came out with a negligee that she slipped softly and transparently on. The smooth silk picked up the sharp tilt of her shoulders in the dressing table mirror. They didn't move as she walked forward and seated herself on the stool and bent into the mirror to plan another campaign of change and perfection. She put on the Cyclax foundation cream first and smoothed it with long, sensual fingers into her face. She half smiled at herself, tilted her head briefly to one side and reached for the blue-green eye shadow. Her body felt wanted.

MARK DACKS PICKED up the sealed envelope from his bed and turned it over. He saw that it was addressed to Mr M Dacks, Casino Hotel, Victoria Falls. There was no stamp on the envelope. The letters had been typed in very small print. He took the flat, hunting knife from the holster beneath his shirt, accurately thrust the point into the un-gummed gap and slit it open with one back-flip of his wrist. He pulled out and unfolded an unlined sheet of white, expensive paper with two typed paragraphs addressed to 'Dear Mr Dacks'. The letter was not signed and wished him nothing faithfully nor sincerely at the end. He read:

> “*To begin with we didn't think you'd last. Amateurs rarely do. There seemed to be no point in making more than surface enquiries and we didn't even bother to find out your name. Word in Africa spreads fast and lately we have found some of our sources of supply getting their stones through to your route. The people you deal with and the people we deal with have both been making money but we have not. This is very wrong.*
>
> *The drop from the top of Devil's gorge to the rocks*

below is 323 feet. At one a.m. in the morning the distance doesn't change. Finding out who you are has cost us a lot of money. You are not an amateur and will be treated accordingly if you keep your appointment tonight. The field in which we operate in Central Africa is very specialised and requires all the resources of one group only. I'm so sorry to spoil your little game but the BSAP appear unlikely to do so in the near enough future.

HE PUT the letter back on the bed so that it looked up at him from its open page. He ran a strong hand through his almost black hair that had never needed more than a little hair tonic to keep it in place. A crooked smile spread over his face. It changed to an expression of hopeful conjecture. A second glance at the envelope sent a run of excitement through the length of his body that built itself up into a bubble of mirth that started in the pit of his stomach and came out of him to echo around the air-conditioned room. There is no fame like infamous fame, concluded the conscious part of his mind, while the undercurrent of himself began imperceptibly to wind itself up for whatever was ahead. He knew that even in the best organised tribes there was always someone who would sell out for sufficient money. Mark Dacks wondered who this now richer person could be. There had never been more than one person in each kraal who had made contact with him and only his personal friends had assisted him, like Korina, in getting it out and covering up the flow of money. If this letter-writer had found him out then why hadn't the police as well? He perceived that his message would go back down the line and that this richer person would leave the home of his forefathers for exile but this didn't solve the immediate problem.

He had never been foolish enough not to realise that other people were also engaged in the transfer from Central Africa of precious stones without the knowledge of the various customs officials whose job it was to prevent such illicit trades, but he had always thought his source of supply lay outside the known channels. Rereading the letter, it became obvious to him that someone had injected stolen diamonds from, most likely, the big diamond fields of South Africa and the Congo into his more peaceful stream of mutually benefiting trade that up until then had caused no one pain, apart from a small amount to himself over that one lost suitcase at Victoria Station. He smiled again at the idea of once more inflicting acute injury on the monopolists, but this was soon lost to a frown when he remembered that somebody was using him, Mark Dacks, to further their own financial gain in a system that up until that very moment he had thought to be a co-operative society with Mark as the well-paid boss.

He looked at his watch and was reassured. There was still an hour before he had to play host to his little tour group. There was time enough for him to think. 'Yes, it has been too easy,' he thought to himself. But then he hadn't started the project with ease and comfort in mind. If this had been his aim he would have plugged into the many diverse routes of deflecting money from the happy, willing public in a way more correctly referred to as 'business'.

When he reached Devil's Gorge later that night he would have the opportunity of resolving the immediate problem of discovering who it was that wished to see him drop 323 feet without a parachute. He folded the letter, took out his wallet and pushed the expensive sheet of paper behind his wad of Portuguese currency so that it was in front of the record card that showed the present weight and value of the stones in his custody. These were due to be moved to London with any further additions at the end of the current Safaris tour, with the unknown assistance of his passengers and fellow travelling companions, who were currently preparing themselves, beautifying themselves, or so he hoped, for their gambling dinner. The thought of food reminded him that he hadn't been able to enjoy a drink that evening without an ulterior motive.

He moved across to his wardrobe, selected a white tuxedo with cream lapels, a black cummerbund, cream trousers, black suede shoes, black socks and a very thin tie, and carried them to the bed and laid them out. He glanced out of the window at the dark on his way to the private bathroom.

He was pleased to see on going inside, a large, clean towel on the rail ready for his use. He stripped methodically, spurred on by the thought of the bar, and walked across into the white-tiled shower recess and turned the cold tap to full with his chin looking up at the little holes in the cylindrical spray. He was quickly rewarded and enjoyed the flood of cold water over his body. He stood under the gushing water for a full half-minute, then shut off the tap and stepped out of the dripping wet shower. The towel gripped the water on his body and he dried quickly, feeling the heat come back despite the air-conditioning.

He dressed with more serious thoughts in his mind and allowed the jumble of facts from the previous eight years to filter into their required places. The thin tie finally looped itself down hungrily from the collar of his white shirt and achieved the nonchalant angle he was always at such pains to achieve. A flick with the stiff brush finished the art of modern sophistication. He dropped his wallet inside his coat pocket.

Opening the door, he walked out on to the thick pile of the red carpet that led him down the corridor to the main, circular staircase. He walked down slowly, giving each person in the reception well below him a searching investigation. A Zimbabwe Bird made the central piece of the marble floor below. The bird was in green with ruby eyes and accepted the treading feet without any apparent pain.

He walked off the last step onto the marble floor and strode across the tail of the twelve-foot mythological bird on his way to the more material pleasures of the bar. The sex-inviting girl at the reception desk caught his eye. He raised one eyebrow, imperceptibly to anyone but her, found she had nothing to communicate other than sex and joined her smile to one of his as he stretched his right hand for the glass door. Inside, he made for the empty barstool beside Mrs Hall and the many bottles that grew nearer as he shortened the gap between himself and a gin sling of the kind he always drank in the heat. He nodded a greeting to the barman.

"Did you find the martini to your satisfaction, Mrs Hall?"

"Hello, Mr Dacks. Please sit down. Yes I'm afraid I did and I've been a little naughty as this is the second one already."

"There seems little left in your glass to give you solace. Joseph, can I have a martini for Mrs Hall as well? I'll take one of those packets of thirty First Lord. Now, Mrs Hall, tell me how you are enjoying yourself. I hope we are looking after you properly."

"Everyone says it is so much better than they had ever really expected. I had heard, of course, that the trip was worth every penny, but I never imagined it really would be but so far it has. The Falls are so beautiful. What time do they switch on the lights tonight?"

"They floodlight the eastern cataract only for an hour after eight as they did last night. There was a lot of talk of spoiling nature so the whole Falls were left for the while. Myself, I think they look superb and the power of falling water is even more magnificent in the arc-lights. No one will ever take away the awe from the 'smoke that thunders'. Thank you, Joseph. How's that for a well-made cocktail?"

He stripped the cellophane wrapping from his new box of First Lord in one movement, opened the box, turned over the smooth flap of silver paper to expose the cylindrical symmetry of the thirty cigarettes, then offered them to Mrs Hall by pressing the open flap of the silver paper down against the open lid with his thumb so that a line of fresh cigarettes rose to her reach. He flicked his Ronson lighter into life as he put the pack on the bar and took one for himself.

"Thank you," Mrs Hall said as he lit her cigarette.

He raised his gin sling towards her new martini, smiled a salute and took an enquiring sip. Satisfied, he drank more fully. This time, there were no marks cut into the inside of his glass, but then none were expected. He sipped again and replaced the glass on the bar.

His eyes flicked to the bar mirror as the door behind him opened. Without moving a muscle he watched Francine Mure walk up behind him. He lost her reflection briefly behind an advertisement for Life cigarettes and then she reappeared in the mirror wearing the difficult combination of a low and sophisticated dress. He got off the high stool and offered it to her with a friendly pat on its seat.

"How did you know I was behind you?"

"The mirror and your perfume. I recognised both. And what can I buy you to drink?"

"A gin and tonic should help."

The double raise of his right hand resting innocently on the bar was sufficient notice for Joseph to turn his back on the customer as he poured the gin and to precipitate two tots into a long glass before turning back with the tonic bottle already upside-down and emptying into the glass. Three drops of angostura bitters and a half slice of lemon followed the Indian tonic water before the whole was passed to Mark Dacks's right hand for onward transmission. He thanked Joseph in Ndebele and added a little more for the measure of the evening, having first satisfied himself that the two other members of the bar were not indigenous. He did this by the simple expedient of deciphering their American drawl. The other drinkers had drifted out to change for the big evening of food and gambling ahead of them all. Mark Dacks savoured another encounter between his gin sling and his palate and began to look forward to one o'clock with a more certain relish.

Harold Ackit appeared in the mirror behind the bottle of green Chartreuse liqueur and joined them. Seeing that there were now too many of them to talk easily at the bar, Dacks guided his guests to a low copper table that supported a dish of piri-piri ground nuts, a bowl of olives and a tray of assorted canapés.

The wicker chairs were surprisingly comfortable and cool. As the ladies seated themselves, Herman Small, in a badly fitting, cold-climate dinner jacket, held open the door for a superbly dressed Anna Featherstone. A waiter materialised beside Dacks, wrote down the new order and gave him a chit to sign for what they had already drunk. The content of Mrs Hall's next drink was directed to be thinner than the first, since otherwise, he conjectured, she would not enjoy her dinner or the sight of so many people losing so much of their money with so much alacrity. The waiter went to the bar and Joseph put the required beverages onto his copper tray. The waiter returned to the table and the assortment was separated into waiting hands.

Herman Small accepted his cold Lion lager with anticipated pleasure, then watched Anna take a sip from her sherry. As he did so, he caught a glimpse of himself in the mirror below and behind a bottle of Charter gin and again decided that it was time for him to do something about his mode of dress. He'd make sure to speak to his father when he returned to London to obtain enough funds to transform himself into a miniature replica of Mark Dacks. He glanced back to the girl and quickly away again as his eyes unexpectedly met hers. He decided that even though her face may perhaps not be the image of perfection, her figure was certainly to be desired. It left little to the growing, determined, resolutely dirty little mind of Herman Small. He looked forward to maturing with the same assurances as the man next to him in the white tuxedo. Mrs Hall, engaging Anna in conversation with apparent enthusiasm, enabled him to study in detail the top surface of his immediate point of interest. The double bulge of the firm young bosom was almost too much for him.

Mark Dacks got up and pulled a chair between Herman and Harold Ackit so that Korina could sit down in a cheongsam dress that showed off her flat hips and the fullness of her bosom. He would like to have talked his new problem over with her, but perhaps it was better kept to himself and Joseph, he decided. They looked quickly at each other and then separated, one back into the company he was with and the other his tasks.

Francine Mure was comfortably accepting the inevitability of the evening and looking forward to its climax. She felt at her strongest in just such a soft-lit corner of a cocktail bar and quickly made herself forget the look Mark Dacks had exchanged with his co-hostess. She was aware of their relationship but didn't imagine this interfering with her plans. She considered him able to look after himself and had no intention of marrying a travel agent, even if he did own his own business. She required money in large quantities and had always considered it unwise to jeopardise the alimony from the previous husband before a suitable financial substitute had been found. She would enjoy seeing the change in his attitude after they had been together. Many men in her past had been indifferent to her sex appeal... Until afterwards. For that reason she always enjoyed her subsequent control over them all the more.

5

DEVIL'S GORGE

Later that evening, while his guests were inside propping up the gaming tables, Mark Dacks stood outside on the veranda considering the best way to play his own particular game. In his case there was no room for chance and losing would not only be the end of him financially but physically as well. He could see two of his guests through the tightly-closed French windows and decided by Francine Mure's expression that she must have won at last. He smiled to himself and only wondered for a moment how long it would take for her to give it all back again to the house.

He turned his back on the tables and listened to the thunder of the Falls some four hundred yards out in front of him. He tried to decide from the rhythm of the pounding water whether they were friendly to him on such a night. Then he turned his wrist so that his watch looked luminously up at him. It was half past twelve in the morning. He looked out further over and away from the Falls, at the moon-bathed epoch of night and knew that there was enough moonlight to show him the way. He flicked the butt of his cheroot over the balcony and watched it fall and bounce off the rocks down below. Sparks flaring out from its lighted end joltingly proclaimed its passage.

He turned back to the French windows and opened one side, to be physically pushed by the cold as he went through into the air-conditioned gaming room. The change in air temperature was over thirty degrees. Unnoticed, he quietly closed the door behind his back, stood for a moment of appraisal, and then walked across to the evening-dressed people seated around the table. They were all desperately concentrating on the newly-spinning wheel and the little black ball of fortune.

He waited for the ball to come to a rest and for Francine Mure's stake to be taken by the croupier before leaning close to her ear. He had decided outside that he must do the job by himself.

"I'll be back in a little while. Look after each other. The tables don't close until four in the morning and sometimes later if the game is good."

"Fine, Mark. I'm determined to win."

"That's the only way to play."

He smiled into her eyes, nodded a farewell to Harold Ackit and moved away towards the big mahogany doors below the Gothic arched main exit from the gaming room. He waved to Mrs Hall playing bridge with three, equally self-sufficient ladies of similar age and means. He was certain that the stakes were high and hoped that she wasn't about to lose too much of her Thomas's money. He glanced sideways at her and was confronted by a frown of knowledgeable concentration that made him reflect that she was more likely to win than to lose.

He pulled at the wrought-iron handle of the well-balanced door and swung it open. He went outside and shut it behind him. There was only the night receptionist at the desk. The marble floor and green Zimbabwe Bird were free of treading feet.

He smiled at the girl as he crossed the open floor and was rewarded by a frown of 'don't touch the samples'. He let out a suppressed 'hic' as he watched her impassive face and was pleased to see it change to disgust. He swung his head round at her in a half drunk circle and fired a well-controlled wink before opening the main door and passing out into the swelter of the African heat and night.

He looked up at the stars from the top of the steps and then moved down them quickly one at a time. He took the well-trodden path towards the rainforest.

His eyes grew accustomed to the night and his ears separated the night noises from the millions of tons of Zambezi water thundering over the Falls and into the gorge. Thousands of pounding years had gutted the softer rocks and gouged the new, lower level of the river bed that wound its way at the bottom of the canyon, in and around the hard rock that had withstood the ages of time.

The violence drew nearer and the wind drifted some of the 'smoke' to settle on him. His hair glistened with the fine droplets of spray but he walked deeper into the riotous vegetation that had never been dry. Puddles appeared on the path that reflected the moon and showed the plops of river water that dripped from the over-hanging trees and hit the surface of moon-shone pools. His wet tuxedo reflected some of the moon and his passage could have been easily marked.

He forked left away from the heart of the thunder and the vegetation began to thin and the spray to subside. Looking downstream, the Falls were on his right along the path to Devil's Gorge.

The spray drifted thinner and then stopped altogether.

He put his hand into his pocket and pulled out a dry box of cigarettes, dried three fingers of his right hand on the silk handkerchief inside his breast pocket and then selected himself a cigarette. His lighter responded to his first flick and the hooded light flared and showed the hollows of his face for a moment. His expression was relaxed and confident. He quickened his pace but the sound of his feet was softer than before. The echo of fallen water resounded in his ears from the depth of the gorge. The moon whispered among the giant spray to his left as it hung over the pounding cauldron. It seemed to be stationary but constantly fell and replaced and fought with itself. The humidity was suffocating.

He stopped thirty yards short of the path that led to the steps in the rocks. The steps went on down to the bottom of Devil's Gorge. They were slippery and badly cut and dangerous even in daylight. He selected a large boulder and seated himself comfortably to wait. His nerves concentrated on giving him the maximum sense of feeling but any passer-by would have cast him aside as a moon-gazer under the spell of the Falls, smoking his last but one cigarette of the day and planning a game flight over Bechuanaland for the following morning. A policeman would have been fooled just as easily.

To confirm any such suspicion, Mark Dacks 'hicced' quietly but rhythmically into the thundering night and finally, as if in great need, twisted himself over on the rock and fished a flask from his hip pocket, removed the stopper with difficulty and swigged methodically at the Oude Meester brandy.

There would have been little doubt in any watching person's mind that among his other stupidities was an over-indulgence in spirits. They would most certainly have cast him off as another rich tourist of no consequence, who was used to wetting an impeccably tailored tuxedo in exchange for a little water to freshen the lost effect of his after-shave lotion.

With finality he thumped the stopper into the bottle. He rolled over again and fumbled the flask back into his pocket, then tried, apparently without success, to sit up straighter. His cigarette rolled out of his fingers and bumped its way off down the side of the rock. He clutched dangerously but by that time it was well and safely out of his reach. He fumbled in his jacket pocket and pulled out the required cardboard box, got his fingers inside among the silver paper and drew out yet another cigarette. He flashed the lighter methodically for some seconds and then turned the cigarette round so that the charred end of the filter-tip was in his mouth. Three more flashes of light produced a red glow at the end of his First Lord and a large moon-filled cloud of smoke above his head.

An animal howl from some few yards behind him was followed by a violent roar that sent a stab of real fear down the vertebrae of his back and which prompted him to hook the flask out of his hip pocket again and remove the stopper with alcoholic speed. The upturned bottle remained above his throat for some moments and was only jerked away by a repeat of the chilling howl of the unknown prey. The deep, resonant roar from further to his left froze him to the rock while the flask still shook uncontrollably in his right hand. The successive roars drew nearer to the steps leading down to Devil's Gorge and the final, petrified howl of the prey echoed in terror above the crash of water going over the edge to eternity.

A small man weaved his way at full speed along the path from the Gorge away from the roaring lion. He looked neither to right nor left. Mark Dacks smelt his fear. He watched him disappear into the night and rainforest before raising one eyebrow in a farewell salute. The lion gave a final roar.

Dacks thumped the stopper into his flask of brandy once again and with surprising agility and accuracy jumped off the rock on to the path and hurried in the direction of the last two animal noises. There was a smile on his face. He reached the incline that led to the steps and walked down with confidence between the rocks that reached high above him on either side. There was just room for his shoulders. The passage had been made in something AD by a split in the rockface caused by too much weight overhanging the big drop. There was a similar, less known and less easily navigated path along a ledge on the side open to the Falls that had a towering rockface on the right-hand side and nothing on the left. Both entrances led to the man-made steps that Mark Dacks began to climb down one at a time. A green slime had grown on the rocks.

The steps led him around in the direction he knew well. He bent himself almost double and went in under the cascading water. The water rushed desperately past him just above his head and down over his shoulders. One touch of the shooting water would have jerked him out into the Falls. He put his hand deep into a crevice some three feet away from the wall of water and drew out a pouch of the same type, size and shape that had recently swam with him across the Zambezi. The pouch fitted into his other pocket and matched the bulge made by his cigarette box.

He turned himself round carefully in the limited space between rock and water and felt the water sucking at his coat. He edged slowly forward, pressing against the shiny rock on his left. He moved out from under the water and began the return climb, step by step, using hands and feet to feel the rock surface for precipitous slime.

Almost with regret he reached the path. He felt his right, wet shoulder, smiled to himself, then felt the left, which was covered in slime. Then he walked quickly away from Devil's Gorge.

The night was silent except for the pounding water. Moving quickly, he followed the path through the rainforest, ignoring the spray and puddles, then took the fork towards the hotel, whose lights were staring out at the dark thunder of the Falls.

He went round to the rear of the building, checked that no one else was around, then silently but with speed began to climb the metal rungs of the fire escape.

He reached the unobtrusive white-painted door that led into the first floor, took a key from his pocket and unlocked his way into the dark building, as he was doing so speculating the craziness of hotels with fire escapes and doors that were always locked.

Inside, with the fire-escape door shut behind him, he opened the door on his immediate right and walked into his own bedroom and through to the bathroom, where he emptied his pockets and shed the clothes that were wet and with slimy-green in too many places into the bath.

Stepping under the shower, he turned on the cold tap and removed the remaining slimy signs of the Falls from his face and hands. After showering, he rinsed the green from his tuxedo in the bath, then hung it on the back of the bathroom door, beneath his dressing-gown.

He moved into the bedroom and across to his wardrobe, selected an identical set of clothes to the ones he had sat down in at dinner and rapidly dressed. Then he laid a case marked *With the compliments of Safaris Limited, Salisbury, Rhodesia* on the bed, opened it and carefully removed its false bottom. The greens and reds glittered and glowed in the poor light and the stones looked well against the soft pad of their white cotton wool. He poured the contents of the new pouch on to an empty patch of the cotton wool, then expertly turned each stone over. He was pleased to see that his trust had again been rewarded. Even without the final confirmation of the experts in London, he was convinced by the beauty and perfection of the emeralds. He put the false bottom, with its underbelly of cotton wool, back into the case and re-waxed the hairline seams around the case's interior to disguise its secret contents once more before closing the lid and clicking the locks back into place. Finally, he collected his pen and wallet from the bathroom, took his record sheet from inside the crocodile skin holder and marked the card with the estimated weight and wealth of the new additions.

Satisfied with his night's work, he flicked the lid of his cigarette box open and took out a First Lord, lit his cigarette in one draw, then put the box in his pocket with the lighter. At the door, he pressed his ear to the wood to listen for passers-by before opening it a crack, then looked out at an empty corridor, stepped into the silence and rapidly closed the door behind him with his left hand while opening the fire escape door with the other.

On the stairs outside, he locked the door behind him and silently moved down the iron rungs. The moon was on the other side of the building. He was in lightless shadow. He kept the glow of his cigarette hidden by the cupped palm of his right hand.

At the bottom of the ladder, he kept in shadow and worked his way around to the front of the hotel and the steps that led him up to the main entrance, whose doors he opened after considerable fumbling and noise. Finally he had them open and greeted the receptionist with a leer and a second wink that seemed to impress her even less than the first.

He walked across the marble floor to the gaming room where the orchestra was still playing. As he closed the door behind him, he glanced at his watch, which told him he'd been away for twenty-three minutes.

6

THE FULL CIRCLE

Francine Mure and Harold Ackit were still watching the roulette wheel but by this time Mrs Hall had one of her bridge companions in the corner bar and had changed her drink to a lager.

'The full circle,' thought Mark Dacks with amusement. He flexed his shoulders and with a smile of greeting walked across to the table and his source of amour for the evening. Both of the gamblers looked up as their stakes were retrieved by the croupier. Francine Mure's disappointment changed to pleasure as he seated himself next to her at the table.

"Try your luck, Mark."

"Yes, I think I will. Tonight seems to be a lucky night. One throw and then we'll all go and have a bottle of champagne. Wine in the heat is good for circulating the blood."

The croupier called for stakes and Mark Dacks passed him a five pound note in exchange for five plaques. He put them all on the seven, having decided that he felt both good and greedy and because two bottles of champagne with brandy were more in keeping with his mood.

The table had four empty places and by the looks on the faces of the people occupying the other twelve, he felt sure that the house had made a considerable profit for one night.

The wheel spun and the small, black ball was tossed with expert fingers into the revolving disk where it cavorted from side to side, going in and equally rapidly coming out of an assortment of black and red coloured numbers up to nine. He smiled encouragement to Francine Mure, who was still persisting with her third husband's money on the black. His smile changed to consolation when the little black ball tripped into seven, a red.

He collected his forty pounds in five pound notes and guided them away from the table across to the gothic doors, ignoring Harold Ackit's nod towards the second discreet bar in the room, which was being tended by two young girls in bathing costumes, both of whom looked bored and tired.

"Joseph will be back on duty in the cocktail bar and he's the only one in the hotel who knows how to mix a champagne cocktail," he said. "I know he soaks lumps of sugar in angostura bitters and I know he uses Oude Meester brandy, but even with just such a wealth of knowledge I can't make them like he does."

He opened the Gothic door and saw them both through before following. They crossed the marble floor and he tried to look as though he was trying not to look drunk. Judging by the glare he received from the night receptionist, he was sure he had been successful.

Once inside the bar, Dacks straightened up and was more than pleased to see Joseph in his customary place. He winked and just a flicker of a smile spread for a second on Joseph's face, before being replaced once again by the inscrutable blankness of the perfect barman. Joseph looked nothing like a lion nor a jackal, but that hadn't mattered in the dark of the rainforest. Dacks allowed the briefest of chuckles to build up in his belly as he remembered the small, European man sent to push him to the bottom of Devil's Gorge fleeing in fear. The laughter died when he remembered that in all probability the man who had written such a charming letter on such expensive notepaper would by now have heard all about the incident and would already have decided his next move.

He ordered the champagne cocktails and enjoyed the pop of the cork and the sight of the bubbly being poured from the neck of such an old bottle on to the treated sugar cubes and brandy. As he expected, the drink was the perfect ending to an interesting evening, and having drained his glass in one movement and had a new one placed within his grasp by Joseph, he was certain that two bottles would only be just sufficient.

"In certain circles they call this drink a Maharajah's chota-peg," he told Francine Mure and Harold Ackit.

"If I hadn't had such bad luck on the table I would try and imagine myself a maharani," said Mrs Mure.

"The secret of that kind of gambling is that one must always expect to lose. The system dislikes such a philosophy aimed at itself and lets you win at first so as to lure you into the trap. The thing is to gamble hard on that first throw and then leave with your winnings. Have another drink. Come along, Harold, drink up. It may never happen. The champagne may lift up your heart."

"If you'll both excuse me, I'll be back in five minutes to drink with you both. Mark, you're an excellent host. My mind was wandering just then to other problems, but you're right and they're not worth thinking about. The next bottle of champagne is on me. You've been buying too many drinks this evening."

"But you forget that I am, in fact, spending your money."

"You won't have much left at this rate."

The three of them laughed as he got off the bar stool. He walked heavily out of the bar. Dacks wondered if Harold Ackit would go into the other bar and proposition one of the bunny girls. He didn't expect to see him back that evening, and concluded that it was his guest's polite way of leaving without spoiling what appeared to be left of the party.

A few minutes later, Francine Mure excused herself and moved across the carpet to the door marked Ladies, leaving Joseph and Mark Dacks alone. With three glasses of good vintage champagne past his throat, Dacks slapped the bar with his right hand, made a resounding crack and doubled up sideways in mirth whilst at the same time trying hard to control the guffaws of laughter that were welling up from the very soles of his feet. Joseph had the same problem, only with more pain caused to his stomach muscles as he was also trying to speak.

"When I... When I... When I get in down that ledge for the last time... I can see him sitting on that first step... And he's so frightened he can't just even move 'till I give him that one more roar and that one more howl and then he's off as if someone has picked him up. Did you see him go?"

"He was running very fast... Your grandfather would be proud of you... He was a fine *ngaka* and I think you'll make just as good a witch doctor. It is good your trade teaches you so many things... Maybe it also tells you how to make a cocktail like this? I hadn't thought of it that way. The first roar made me think you were real."

"It was your idea to frighten him off like that."

"Even the bravest killer is frightened of a lion, especially here. He can see a man wanting to attack him and know how to deal with the situation but the lion takes him out of his sphere and he becomes frightened like any other animal. He was right, of course... He wouldn't have been able to protect himself without a rifle."

They meditated upon this hunting problem for some moments and were able to compose themselves enough so that they were able to return from being an *ngaka* and a merchant in illicit stones to being the perfect barman and the perfect host.

Francine Mure re-joined the group and was rewarded by Joseph bubbling further champagne into a new glass on top of the angostura bitters-treated sugar and brandy. She felt both full and expectant. She enjoyed the feeling of chrome and mirrors and well-lit, interesting bottles around her to the full. It was the prelude to her satisfaction. For her this feeling of sophistication was deeply mingled with sex. She hoped that Harold Ackit would not return. She had been pleased to see his chair still vacant when she opened the door of the Ladies and looked out from behind the repaired mask of her new face.

She turned herself discreetly on the high stool to make herself more comfortable and to liberate a little more of the newly sprinkled perfume that filtered delicately and immediately into the waiting nostrils of her appreciative escort.

Mark Dacks took the box of First Lord cigarettes from the right-hand pocket of his white tuxedo, which showed not a sign of creasing despite the heat, flicked open the lid and offered her the box, and was no longer surprised to watch her accept the offer. He carefully selected one for himself and put the dual charcoal filter into his mouth. The trace of a frown appeared above the black eyebrows and the steel blue eyes measured themselves with the problem seeping into his mind. He had no intention of taking his lady companion up to his or anyone else's room, as he had decided some years before that satisfied women in his particular trade were more of an impediment than an asset. While they still wanted, they still complied.

His mind travelled back to Devil's Gorge and once again he tried to put himself into the other person's body, the person who had discovered the information he'd thought had only been written on the inside of his now shattered glass. The carrier, he was sure, would be as much concerned as himself with the problem of handing him the emeralds privately and receiving the negotiable currency in Zambian pound notes. This person could have been bribed, but again would he not have disappeared immediately instead of leaving his pouch in the rocks as arranged in the event of an emergency, when the rules dictated that he should come back the next day for the money put in the same place by Joseph? The tribe had ways of dealing with traitors that were certainly unpalatable for those watching but even more painful for the victims. Then there was exile in a world that pays for ability and services and gives nothing for nothing in return. He thought again. There could have been a leak or the long association between himself and Joseph marked down and Joseph followed when the transfer was being made. The nights were dark and the trees had long ears. He concluded that there must have been a great deal of planning and patience leading up to the letter. He tried to consider their next move and found too many possibilities in his mind to give any one of them certainty.

He took his champagne glass from the bar, raised it to Francine Mure and converted his frown to a smile of confidence. She returned his gesture and they both drank it down and with a spasm of intimate laughter put their glasses back on the bar simultaneously.

Joseph slid new cocktails towards them both and Mark Dacks led her again into drinking it down. He put his glass on the bar and took his burning cigarette from the fork of the newly cleaned, copper ashtray and slowly drew a glow into the tip. The smoke pushed down into his lungs. He didn't look at Joseph but felt the other's satisfaction nonetheless. A smile hovered in the crow's feet at the sides of Dacks's eyes as the expectancy in Francine Mure's eyes evaporated and was replaced by a film of potential sleep. The sparkle had gone. The hour of night had caught up with her.

"I suddenly feel tired, Mark. Must be all the drink. Do you mind if I go to bed? Funny this, normally I can go on all night."

"Most likely it's the altitude. It affects people in the end. Some get used to it after a few months. I'm tired myself. I'll see you upstairs."

He took a strong hold of her elbow and helped her off her stool. Together they moved to the glass door.

"Goodnight, Joseph. You won't have any more customers tonight, so why not close the bar. Your cocktails are still as good as ever."

He had a slight slur in his voice in preparation for the girl at the reception desk.

"Goodnight, Mr Dacks. I hope you have pleasant dreams."

He opened the heavy glass door and walked Mrs Mure out into the round hall. They crossed it methodically. As he passed the watching girl he slowly swivelled his drunken head, popped his eyes at her and twisted his face into a lecherous leer that seemed to be meant for any old female who liked any old Dacks in any old white tuxedo.

They began to navigate the staircase. With the increasing weight of Francine Mure, he was acutely glad of his sobriety. He weaved them higher, stair by stair. At the last bend he looked down on to the reception desk and was rewarded by a sight of the girl gaping up at his face. He lifted an apparently heavy hand from the banister and gave her a wave before going on up slowly and out of her sight.

He took his drugged companion to the door of her room and turned the handle, keeping her steady with the other hand. The door swung open. He groped for the light-switch and turned it on.

"I don't know why I'm so tired. I'll be fine now. Pity really, but it doesn't matter. There'll always be another time."

They chuckled at their own joke as he seated her firmly on her bed and withdrew. He waved in dejection and went out into the silent corridor, closing her door behind him. He paused amidst the stillness of the night and appreciated that the dryness in his mouth was due to an excess of Maharajah's chota-peg. The effort and heat had drawn drops of perspiration from the crease marks on his forehead. He glanced at his watch without lifting his arm and decided that a few hours' sleep, all that was left of the night, were what he needed.

He walked on down the thick pile of the carpet under the nightlights of the corridor. He made no sound as he reached the last room on the left and paused with his right hand halfway to the handle. He listened again and was convinced that someone was inside and that that someone was not Korina Prague. His guest was moving around the room. A cupboard opened then clicked shut. He waited tense and motionless, deciphering the sounds. There was no light under the door and no reason for anyone to be inside at two-fifteen in the morning. He turned the door handle without making a sound but the door didn't open. It was locked.

Stealthily moving across to the fire-escape door, unlocking and opening it, he went out on to the iron-grille landing. On the other side of the railing, running away from him across the length of the wall was a brick ledge protruding seven inches from the side of the hotel. Some feet above this, Mark Dacks studied the eaves of the roof and the wooden rim that lipped over like a pelmet from under the last line of the tiles. He was confident that the ledge went out to the corner of the building and around to the other side and to the window that looked straight into his bedroom. But it was too dark for him to be absolutely certain.

Buttoning the jacket of his tuxedo, flexing his fingers and without any further thought put his right leg up to the iron rail, his left hand on the wall face and pushed himself up sharply into a standing position.

He got his hands in under the eaves and closed his fingers firmly on the wooden pelmet, relieved it was not crumbling from white ants. Looking down he estimated there was a two-and-a-half-foot drop to the thin line of protruding bricks. Beyond that was a sixty-foot drop to a tarmac path. He shuddered.

Concentrating he dropped his one foot onto the ledge, then the other, his fingers taking some of the weight, his back against the rough plastered wall. Inching along he began the shuffle along the ledge. The heat and tension were pulsating through his body whilst his mind forced him along. Looking out at the night with the pale light of the moon he heard the pounding of the Falls and hoped he would not be observed.

The pain was building in his calf and stomach muscles from the pressure of holding his body flat against the wall. Then the problem of getting around the corner of the building loomed. Glancing to his left, there were six more feet to go to the corner: focusing he tried to relax his body.

Cautiously he continued on where he forced himself to push away with his hands and to fall diagonally across the corner of the building. Hanging like a taut bow his stomach felt violently heavy. Probing with his left foot around the corner, Dacks found a similar ledge facing the Falls, the relief overwhelming.

Perilously swivelling away and around on to the new ledge, his sinews tightened with the first sign of fear. He was now facing the wall, clinging to the wooden pelmet, his heels hanging over the ledge. Looking like a spider he began to move sideways towards the unlit window. The spider, thrown into indistinguishable relief by the pale light of the moon, drew closer and finally stopped next to the window.

The side of the window gave a firm grip enabling Dacks to bring his face across to peep into his bedroom. He was not surprised to see a concentrated line of light made by a pencil torch, but he was concerned when he realised the light's direction. The beam ended at the lock of the case marked *With the compliments of Safaris Limited, Salisbury, Rhodesia.*

The window was firmly shut, but not locked, to take advantage of the air-conditioning inside. He had known this from the outset. At the same time that he drew his thin-handled, thin-bladed knife from its sheath against his chest, another, even finer knife, was produced inside the darkened room and inserted in the lock of the case. Mark Dacks could feel his chest beating against the wall in front of him. He fitted his knife under the bottom of the sash window and the increasing pressure finally shifted the wooden frame upwards. The millions of gallons of water going over the Falls behind him drowned out the noise he was making. He waited, but the man inside was still intent on the only locked case in the room.

Dacks balanced himself and got the tips of his fingers of his right hand under the window. He waited, jerked the window up and pulled himself over the sill and was just in time to land in a pair of outstretched arms that had been momentarily startled from their work. The two bodies fell over the case and crashed to the ground with Dacks ending expertly on top with the tip of his knife pointing just below the intruder's chin. A sharp thrust would have taken the Swedish steel blade right through into the lock-picker's brain.

Dacks chuckled. "I don't remember inviting you to my room so late in the night," he said down the blade of his knife.

"I have a search warrant."

"So had Brutus, for he was an honourable man... And I believe my grandmother had a similar document."

"I'm a police officer."

"So was my grandmother."

"I'll book you for that knife."

"You'll be doing very little indeed in the future if you don't tell me what you're doing in my room behind a locked door."

"Are you Mark Dacks? It's too dark to see a bloody thing."

"Funny thing, but this happens to be his room and he's not in the habit of breaking into private citizens' bedrooms."

"I went to school with Mark Dacks at Plumtree. It's Jimmy van Niekerk's throat that you're so determinedly thrusting that knife at."

"I haven't seen him for fifteen years. Yes, they tried their best to educate Mark Dacks at Plumtree. Where have you been hiding so long to appear suddenly out of history in my bedroom? A very unlikely coincidence."

"It's what happens to police officers when they stick to country stations. They move from one bush station to another and come into towns like foreigners. No one hears of them again. Now as an old and newly established friend, will you let me up to turn on the light and show myself? Then we can have the kind of talk that will answer a number of questions for both of us."

"Why didn't you ask those questions to my face downstairs?"

"Because I thought they were a lot of rubbish and better investigated quietly to complete the records and then forgotten about. Now, will you let me up?"

"I'm quite happy asking the questions like this but since you ask so nicely there seems no point in being discourteous."

Puzzled, Dacks moved off his 'old friend' but kept the knife in front of him. The blade showed up clearly in the colourless beam of the moon.

He edged backwards to the door and groped successfully for the light switch, plunging them both into the brightness of electric light. Jimmy van Niekerk wore a defensive smirk. The dark eyebrows of Mark Dacks rose fractionally as he replaced his knife in its sheath and gave his hand to the man lying on his back on the floor with his elbows deep in the pile of an imitation Persian carpet that would have fooled anyone but an expert. Dacks pulled his school companion to his feet.

He walked over to a cupboard, opened it and was pleased to see that it showed few signs, if any, of being rifled. He put his right hand into the back of the left-hand compartment and pulled out a half-full bottle of his favourite Oude Meester brandy.

He walked back with it around the silk-counterpane bed to the highly-polished mukwa bedside cabinet that showed the grain of the indigenous wood to perfection. He pressed the catch and the well-oiled door folded back to reveal a small array of glasses that sparkled to the shine of the light. There were three rows of them on a glass shelf. He selected two brandy balloons, inspected their cleanliness against the light and, satisfied, put them confidently on top of the cabinet, removed the cork from the brandy bottle with an encouraging plop and poured generous tots into both glasses. The Oude Meester bottle arrived with screw-tops, but Mark Dacks always had them replaced with corks. He considered that brandy and cork breathed better together. He studied the dial on the air-conditioning control and turned it to cold before turning back to his unheralded companion with a large brandy balloon in each large hand.

"Have a drink, even though you say you're on duty."

The hand that passed the drink showed no sign of its previous strain. The outstretched arm was completely rigid. Dacks wondered about his sleep but only for a moment. He offered one of the armchairs to Jimmy van Niekerk, pulled the only other one in the room around from the other side of the bed, seated himself comfortably in front of the self-proclaimed member of the BSAP and stretched his legs to the full.

"Cheers."

"Cheers."

They raised their glasses to each other and threw the normal methods of brandy drinking out of the window, draining their glasses and returning the balloons to their laps with merely a smear of the departed alcohol to tell the tale of the passage of the Oude Meester. Dacks reached for the bottle and emptied an exceptional tot into the other man's glass and treated his own in the same way. They smiled at each other and drank more discreetly. They both laughed loudly, both realised it was just past the middle of the night and controlled themselves. Their mouths opened to speak together and shut again. They drank instead.

"A man's face changes with age but his smile always stays the same," said Dacks.

"I shouldn't have recognised you without looking for a likeness, but having found it there's no mistaking who you are."

"Do you remember leaving our erstwhile housemaster's car sideways at the far end of the main corridor?"

"It took ten of us to lift it."

"Twelve. Towards the end you and I stopped giving expert advice and gave them a hand."

"We had some laughs."

"It was a long time ago. What are you doing in the British South African Police?"

"CID County Districts... At the moment, covering from the Falls down to Wankie and well into the Reserves on either side. Keeps me busy."

"And who or what have I done that is so interesting that it merits your wasting your time in this room?"

"I shouldn't think anything but we had to check up. When I saw the name I thought I'd enquire in person. We often have cranks on the telephone but regulations say they must be investigated, just in case."

"What is it? 'Sergeant' van Niekerk?"

"Inspector. I was lucky. Then again, most people want to be posted to the big cities so I didn't have too much competition. I didn't expect the Mark Dacks the caller referred to would in fact be the one I plotted with at school but stranger things have happened in my last fourteen years with the police."

"Who's 'the caller'?"

"Some guy who refused to give his name but was adamant that you had a pouch full of emeralds in your room that you wouldn't be able to explain away."

The laughter grew inside Dacks and as it burst out in crashing mirth he forgot all about the time of the night or the dreams of his tourists in the adjacent rooms. The noise subsided and made expectant room for more brandy. He leaned forward again with the bottle, topped up the inspector's glass then did the same to his own.

"So that's what you were looking for. I hope you found some. I could do with a pile of emeralds for my old age."

"I made a good search but, and I would say fortunately, found nothing. I didn't get a chance to look in that case, if you remember."

Dacks got up, realised why the air-conditioning was having the opposite effect, and closed the window by pushing the open half down to meet the sill, then picked up the suitcase, fished a bunch of keys from his trouser pocket, inserted one in the lock and flicked open the catch and handed it over.

"Be my guest."

The Inspector turned his eyes from Dacks to the case, lifted up the lid and looked into the empty case, then shut the lid and put the case down on the carpet beside him with a small, uncontrolled mark of relief that wasn't lost on Dacks.

"I was wasting my time with the knife," said the policeman.

"So was I. I thought you were a burglar."

"Why do you carry a concealed knife like that anyway? Just as well we know each other or I might have to pinch you on that."

"Protection, Jimmy. I'm out in the bush a lot and feel safer with something to use. You never know when a cat's going to jump you, and it's as likely to be with a gun in hand as not. I've made it a habit so I'll never be unprepared. Controlled habit is a good means of security. I'd prefer to carry my .22 but my licence won't let me. A knife is better than nothing."

"What do you do here?"

"Bring in tourists and show them the sights and try, with the help of Korina Prague, to give them that bit more to think about when they get home so that they will interest their friends in an exclusive tour by Safaris. I inject the aura of romance and feeling. I haven't had to advertise once in the eight years I've been running. My guests are sleeping in the rooms off the corridor outside."

"How many?"

"Five on this trip."

"You must charge them a fortune."

"I do. If I bring more than six it becomes like a Cook's tour and the whole idea loses its point. I make as much profit again out of the travel agency in Salisbury but the two go together. The snob name of Safaris (Pvt) Limited makes people book their less snob-like holidays through us. The world's a funny place."

"Who'd want to try and get you into trouble?"

"A competitor or more likely a man whose wife knows me well. It's one of my failings. I can't ignore a good-looking woman. Funny how often the best of them have small men for husbands. A small man would think of a juvenile trick like this in the hope that it would make me embarrassed."

"People are usually frightened to bring the police into their practical jokes."

"Oh come off it, Jimmy. How many times have you people been phoned about bombs in cinemas and plots against visiting statesmen? For every one that kills President Kennedy, ten thousand are nothing but hoaxes."

"That's why I'm here. I hoped to satisfy myself, while you entertained the woman downstairs, and be able to leave without dropping my card. By the way, how did you get in at the window?"

Dacks got up, beckoned the Inspector and opened the window again so they could both look out.

"Good God, Mark, it's too high for a ladder and not even a fly could climb up there from down below."

"I walked along the brick ledge from around the other side of the hotel."

"You must have been crazy to have walked on a ledge that wide."

"I've known of my problem for some years. I enjoyed the walk. Do you mind if I close the window as the heat's coming in again and so are the mosquitoes. By the by, what was I meant to be able to do with the emeralds if I'd found them?"

"There is a very thorough channel that seems to operate right here on the borders of Rhodesia, Zambia and Bechuanaland, so the caller didn't sound so crazy at first."

"Do you know who these people are?"

"No, we don't. We leave it mostly to the South African police as the stones come from South African mines. Some come from the Kivu province of the Congo and a few from Tanzania, but most are from the diamond fields around Kimberley. We caught a few of the African carriers and were able to tell where the stones came from. With a monopoly such as that enjoyed by de Beers, it is not so surprising that an illicit organisation should have grown so strong. They control ninety per cent of the free world's diamonds, most of which come from Africa. These large companies are all doing very well. So far as the price of diamonds is concerned they are necessary to control the flow of stones so that the market isn't flooded and Mrs Jones's twenty-year-old engagement ring suddenly drops in value overnight. They say there are enough surface diamonds on the south-west coast of South Africa to drop the price of diamonds by half. They can be picked up in handfuls off the beach. The whole area is cordoned off and the police and the nature of the surrounding coast discourage visitors.

"So de Beers and their associates have a monopoly that keeps the supply in pace with the demand. With the price so high for such a small object, illegal traffic is rife and difficult to stop. Stealing from the mines themselves can be watched but as the monopolists are not prepared to pay anything for a find inside their concessions, and most of Africa falls under this category, anyone finding a deposit keeps it quiet and tries to sell the stones illegally. This is a vast country and to locate these small diggings is impossible and, though it shouldn't be, some of the police sympathise with these unlucky people and hope that the next find they make will be copper or some other mineral that helps the country and legally helps themselves at the same time. Prospecting is heart-breaking enough without finding something in the middle of nowhere and getting nothing in return, irrespective of the fact that the concessionist would never again find the deposit without that prospector's help. The problem of stolen diamonds doesn't affect us as much as other countries, so we keep our time for the more pressing matters and investigate the illicit trade only when it comes to our notice."

They thought about this for the time it took to drink again.

"Do you still do any shooting?" asked Jimmy van Niekerk.

"Only when one of the customers is interested and then I go out in one of the controlled hunting areas. I grew tired of killing game many years ago. Guns haven't been mentioned by the group we have with us this time. I keep in practice on the range and that's mostly it."

"Can you still hit a spinning shilling with a .22 revolver?"

"Yes."

"You were the star turn of the school with that trick."

"It's not as difficult as it looks."

"You bet!"

"Just practice."

They drank again and drained their glasses.

"I must go."

"Come and have a drink with the party tomorrow. A live CID inspector will add a little glamour to the tour. These people don't lead very exciting lives in the ordinary way. You'll be doing me a favour."

"Put like that I can't refuse."

"Seven-thirty tomorrow. The reception girl will tell you which bar we're in. You're not married?"

"No."

"You'll enjoy yourself."

"Till tomorrow. You not married?"

"Never been able to make up my mind."

Dacks opened the door expectantly for the policeman, who promptly put his glass on the cabinet and patted him on the shoulder as he walked out into the corridor.

Dacks watched him disappear around the corner and smiled. He concluded that a small country, with only one hundred thousand males, of whom probably twenty thousand were within his age group, had its advantages.

He closed the door and felt the tiredness, helped by the brandy and effort he had made in getting into the window, crawl over him. He took off his tuxedo, meticulously hung it on a specially made, wide-shouldered hanger and put it back with its twins in the cupboard. He remembered to have the one behind the bathroom door packed away for delivery to the dry-cleaner in Salisbury and selected himself a pair of maroon silk pyjama trousers from the compartment under the bottles of alcohol. After pulling on the smooth trousers with the frightening colour, he padded across the room to turn off the main light, enjoying a draught of the air-conditioning on his bare back, then returned to the bed in the darkness, pulled back the single sheet and climbed in. Soon, he'd relaxed all the way through his body and mind and dropped into a deep and restful sleep. The Falls continued their never-ending pounding of the rocks a little way away down below his room.

7

WATCHFUL EYES

Anna Featherstone was more conscious than usual of her reflection in the mirror, but was still unaware of the reason. With a few more years, and with some valuable experience behind her, she would jump to the right conclusion immediately. She adjusted the pale blue, soft yet smooth top of her two-piece sunsuit so that it was straight to the matching shorts covering almost to her navel. The firm, revealing outfit was the London fashion for holidays in the Caribbean, Las Palmas and Madeira. She put the final brush to her shoulder-length hair and twisted the ends with a curl and a pat. She was pleased with the shape of her figure, turned herself sideways to the long mirror, stood up, pushed out her chest and pulled in her stomach, turned her head dramatically on to her shoulder nearest to the mirror and rightly concluded that the picture of her just so would successfully grace the pages of a number of glossy magazines.

The pain behind her eyes returned with the tilted position of her head and involuntarily made her hand go to the bottle marked Disprin on her dressing table. She unscrewed the cap with brittle impatience, dropped two pills into a glass and half-filled it from the balloon-shaped bottle of water. The Disprin fizzed as she watched.

She was hypnotised by the fizzing liquid. Her mind lay fixed in a stare.

Finally, she picked up the glass, stirred inside with a long finger, the tip having been cleverly touched up and smoothed over with a colourless nail varnish, bobbing the pills up and down till the white foam of their original form disappeared completely. She then drank the sweet mixture right down. She rolled her large brown eyes in the hope of a reprieve. Her hangover was bad but not as bad as it had been two hours before when she had first awoken. The sun had then defeated the coolness of the air conditioning completely with it streaming in over her bed, onto her hair that spread out over the yellow pillow with its delicate white lacy edges. The sunlight had heated the one sheet with more efficiency than an electric blanket on full heat. The ceiling was no longer going around in the way she had dimly remembered from the previous night, but trying to lift her head and gold-burnished brown hair from the pillow had proved completely impossible. She had lain there for half an hour while pieces of the previous night appeared in her mind and just as suddenly went out again. She had a feeling that they had both been drunk. She had experienced a feeling of guilt, luck and salvation for this duplicity. Apart from her head and stomach, the rest of her body felt quite normal and gave her no cause for alarm.

With the heavy bulge of her breasts still pushing at her from out of her reflection in the mirror, she was able to smile at the evening and remember the parts of it that she had enjoyed. She turned her nose up like a rabbit hoping for food and realised the gesture was meant for Herman Small who was not in the room, for which she was thankful. She twitched her nose at the mirror again and felt a warm feeling in her stomach, that was nothing to do with the alcoholic sediment firmly deposited there, and that was most definitely going sour. She re-inspected her make-up, confirmed its success and looked forward to the day when she wouldn't need so much. It was very much better, than it had been six months before and she hoped that just maybe, the sun would do the rest of the trick for her and confound her daddy's Harley Street skin specialist.

She had been avoiding for years his boring diets, while all the time telling him that sixteen- to eighteen-year-old girls sometimes did have such problems and that nature was best left to take care of itself.

She didn't often have such moods of self-assertion, but when she did they were dangerous, and there was definitely one in her countenance then. It was directed towards an overpowering need to physically tease Herman Small and all his stupid ideas about life, that she hadn't understood and which she didn't wish to make herself miserable about. She liked her power over him and wished to practise it some more. His father was beautifully rich and so the practice would not be misplaced, and if it was misunderstood it wouldn't really matter.

Putting the flats of her hands under the soft blue material of the top of her sunsuit, she lifted them both to see if they looked any better like that. Then she remembered that the lower position permitted the slightest of movements as she walked and it was this, she again remembered, that her friends had all been trying to perfect.

Anna got up, shook her shoulders very demurely to make sure they moved, satisfied herself of this and promptly let in well over one hundred degrees of Fahrenheit temperature. She continued through the door, shutting it carefully behind her so as not to wake up the pains in her head any more than necessary.

She walked down the corridor and felt some of her strength return as her very high heels dug deeply into the pile of the red carpet. At the far end of the line of doors the yellow glow of the mid-morning sun brushed the carpet. She remembered her day was scheduled for an evening game flight into Bechuanaland and hoped that her body by then would feel more inclined to flipping up into the bright-blue sky in a perilously small, most certainly bumpy, light aircraft.

Reaching the stairs and taking a strong hold of the wooden, smoothly-polished banister, Anna solemnly began her descent. She guided herself with her right hand and kept her head on the level by staring rigidly at the bushman murals that were descending the curved wall with her and the stairs. Endlessly, it seemed, she descended from one step to an equally large-sized other, and was only brought up to a stunning halt by her right hand jarring the base of the magnificently-carved elephant head that usually announced to those with sight the end of both the banister and the stairs a little earlier. With difficulty she bent her arm and guided one foot off the thickly carpeted last stair. For a moment there was suspense and then she heard her heel click on the marble floor of the reception well. She got her left foot on to ground level, steadied herself and moved away from the hand support. She tacked round and headed for the plate-glass door into the lounge and was beyond grateful to the waiter who then opened the door to facilitate her rigid mode of travel. Concentrating she held off the uncertainty in her belly.

With her back dead straight she passed through the open door and was greeted by a sheepish man she remembered too well from the previous evening doing more of the gesticulation and less of the staring, less of the black coffee drinking and more of the beer swilling. Her stomach turned just a trifle but was quickly overcome by the desire she had built into it in her bedroom, the desire to assert and overpower and thereby dominate.

"I'm sorry, Anna. It was all my fault. I should not have let either of us drink so much. I hope I wasn't too awful."

"You were. Pour me a cup of coffee without any milk."

"Of course."

"I have one teaspoonful of sugar."

"Of course."

"There's no of course about it."

"Of course."

"Thank you."

"It wouldn't have happened if I hadn't won so much on that confounded table."

They looked at each other and giggled and dipped their faces into their coffee cups as their eyes peeled away from looking at each other. It was the turn of both their stomachs to flip over simultaneously.

Mrs Hall waved to them brightly from an alcove bathed in sunshine that directly overlooked the eastern cataract, where millions of gallons of water was heading to the edge, falling with finality over the Falls at one hundred miles per hour. They both agreed with meaningful looks that Mrs Hall had no right on her consumption of alcohol to be so bright in the mornings.

The coffee cleared some of the worst feeling from Anna's mouth and told her that there was more in her stomach than an empty cavity with small, dried peas inside just left to rattle around. The coffee went down and trammelled the same passage as ten sweet sherries and that frightful and fateful just one last glass of champagne.

Herman watched her just-uncovered navel as she drank, felt her indignant eyes dissecting the direction of his own, but was prevented by his hangover from tearing them away immediately. He raised them a little, stopped at the soft blue bulges of her top, and with difficulty travelled up to the very inviting mouth. His gaze then moved on to the deep-brown eyes, that lost their indignation and took on a softer, more promising aspect of the whole affair, as he stared into them to his fill.

Mrs Hall watched the exchange with a little sadness and ordered herself a dry martini from the waiter, asking him to have it mixed by Joseph in the other bar. The waiter went off on his errand. She looked back at the youngsters and was a little hurt to see they were still looking at each other in exactly the same way. She thought back over her own life and to Thomas, and further still, and time dissolved completely and the memories were quite real.

The smiles were lingering at the corners of her mouth and deep in the old, wise eyes when the waiter returned with her drink and placed it in front of her on the low, highly-polished coffee table under a round, moisture absorbent doily.

She raised the glass and drank to a happy past. She no longer felt envious of the couple walking across the lounge and talking about swimming, reaching the door in step, him pulling it open, letting her go first, his eyes plainly and hopefully watching the hard, youthful firmness barely covered by her shorts.

Mrs Hall sighed at the thought of the expanse she sat upon, blessed the advances in corsetry and addressed herself to the second half of her perfectly mixed dry martini that she knew without asking had been made with Booth's Gin and Noilly Prat vermouth in quantities closely resembling ten parts of the first against one part of the latter.

The power of the hot sun was full on the Falls and reflected brilliantly in the plummeting water. She concluded that it was quite as beautiful for her as it had been for David Livingstone but thought, on reflection, that she saw the whole thing a little better over the rim of just such a martini mixed in just such a way. She took a filter-tipped cigarette from her tortoise-shell case, that had been given to her by Thomas on their second anniversary. She fitted the cigarette firmly into the black, stubby holder that she knew would sift an alarming deposit of nicotine, gripped the Bakelite in her teeth, dashed off a match with skill and lit up. She agreed with herself, as the first cloud of smoke moved up past her grey hair, that the second home of tobacco, Rhodesia, produced the perfect cigarette. She poignantly drew a second time and the smoke went deep into her much maligned lungs. She would have been surprised if anyone had suggested that she might have a hangover. She felt perfectly normal and was enjoying herself to the very full.

THE WATER in the pool was quite still and reflected with calm the over-head rays of the powerful sun. The straight lines of its hard blue edges touched the white tiles, reflecting in the water some six inches of the Roman figures that were lightly sketched on the hard, glossed porcelain that edged the expanse of the top surround of the bath. Surrounding the pool, white-painted filigree iron chairs and garden couches with matching white, clean, strongly piped back and seat cushions, were both cool and inviting under the crimson awnings that flowed out expansively above each of the tables.

Two of the seating areas were occupied by hotel guests in the latest bathing costumes that ranged from a black two-piece joined together with a slither of white netting, to an orange bikini and finally to a girl in an apple-green, tight-fitting one-piece with a backline plunge that only just stopped in time. Ice occasionally clinked in the long sun-splashed glasses, and straws silently jutted out of other, equally cool glasses that stood waiting on round glass-topped tables. The crimson awnings and the green of cucumbers and mint that hung suspended among the clear ice cubes at the top of the frosted glasses, were all reflected on the tables.

Herman Small reached the folded-back glass doors that gave out on to the well-cared for green grass, that led up to the tiled smoothness of the pool, and with difficulty, looked at each group in turn through his dark glasses. He confirmed that she had not yet arrived and tentatively placed his right foot on the hard African grass with trepidation and suspicion, and finally moved out in his natty pair of pink and green-checked bathing trunks. He should never have bought them but, having been purchased, now had to be worn with at least an air of confident ease.

Halfway across the lawn he stopped and studied the rainbow made by the sun in the floating spray of the Falls that rose high above the chasm in the crust of the earth. Silvery spray topped the pure yet mingling colours and seemed to him in his sedimentary alcoholic haze to wash the hot arrows of the sun's rays with coolness and peace. The dust-blue dome of the sky behind the rainbow made a perfect background. For the first time he began to appreciate why it had been called a natural wonder of the world.

He concluded finally that excess alcohol in the sediment of his blood must have increased his sensitivity and all for the good. He looked again at the Falls embraced by the mid-morning sun and received a further feeling of well-being from his association with the pure brilliance of so natural a beauty.

"Stop gaping, everyone is looking at you."

Automatically his feet began to move forward again, carrying him towards the farthest cluster of chairs around an awning and a table, with the urgency of her whisper only half penetrating the inertia of his appreciation.

They reached the chairs in step and stopped within the limits of society's dictates to look again, as this time he was not within the focal point of people sitting in their prescribed places with nowhere else to stare. Normality dictated that the grass was there to be walked across and not to be stood upon and used as a base for staring.

They sat opposite each other and contemplated one another for the first time in the minimum of covering. Their ultimate thoughts were disgustingly similar. She concluded that he was remarkably well-made and that his tailor was certainly in the wrong kind of business. He had a strong urge to touch the pure white soft bikini top that covered her breasts, just, and to halfway up her hips, just, and left him in both instances with the most delightful grounds for speculation and intrigue. He transferred his thoughts to the Falls only to have them transferred back again almost immediately. She had slowly leaned forward and permitted his dirty little imagination to dip down even lower, and for a brief moment of truth to see that the loose-fitting cloth had fallen away leaving them both, strongly and firmly, pointing across the gap between themselves and propriety.

She enjoyed her moment of tease and then sat up straight again with her legs just that fraction apart. Then Mark Dacks walked out of the building with Korina Prague and all eyes around the pool, male and female, including Anna Featherstone's and Herman Small's, focused in two directions, the women's in one and the men's in the other. The size of his shoulders was very pronounced in a bathing costume, and the soft, full curves of her body had the strongest powers of attraction and thought provocation. They both walked to the pool, dropped their towels and then their dark glasses on top of their towels, turned to the water, contemplated its surface for a moment, then dived into the cool blueness of the sky's reflection. Their splash rode momentarily above the thunder of greater, faster water. The crocs in the river upstream and away from the dragging pull to the edge and over no doubt ignored both sounds and merely blinked at the warm, baking sun that was blissfully drying their scales.

As Dacks powered himself down the pool, there was no sign of fatigue or the fact that he hadn't slept for thirty-eight hours.

A small man with an oval four-chinned face watched them all through the double glass window from within the lounge. He was thinking how simple it really was and drank a toast to his thought in the dregs of his coffee. He hated Africa in the same way that he hated most other things in his life, though his particular and most vindictive hatred had always been directed at women, all women, as none of them had ever done anything but laugh at him even in the days when he had had only two chins, which was a very long time ago, practically in his mother's womb.

He would like to have a room full of women all looking like the one blissfully swimming in the cool, pure water some fifty yards away from him on the other side of the large pane of glass that prevented him hearing her splashes. He wanted these women all to be 'willing' for him through their fear of his powers. He savoured the thought and his chins began to shake with his hatred, his small eyes grew smaller and the half-cold coffee shook its way out of the spout of the pot as he poured it and watched it go down to join the old dregs in his cup. As the small cup came up to his fleshy mouth his round little eyes focused on the firm, almost transparent cloth covering a small portion of Korina Prague's rear as she pulled herself out of the water. The coffee stopped at the restriction in his throat and he began to choke and liberally spill coffee all over himself.

8

A BIRDS-EYE VIEW

The Cessna 172 dipped a wing in half salute and flew out over Bechuanaland away from Rhodesia. The pounding spray and the big river had been left behind some minutes before and all that the three passengers and pilot could see down below was dry, slightly swaying elephant grass and the brown tops of stunted trees. It was game country. The plane headed towards small, triangular dots that grew more and more like giraffes as the heads, long necks, chunky bodies and spindly long legs drew closer. Some three miles west of them, and flying in the strong glint of the late afternoon sun, Dacks could make out the other aircraft that was carrying his second load of tourists. There had been no real need for him to come but Harold Ackit had insisted, pointing out that there was one spare seat and that they would then be able to talk about the flight on equal terms afterwards. Then, after all, Harold Ackit had decided to go with Francine Mure, and as Mrs Hall was already in that aircraft, there had been nothing for him to do but to climb into the second Cessna next to the pilot, with Herman Small and his new girlfriend sitting behind.

Dacks considered the bush below and the fact that he hadn't had enough sleep in the past two days. He yawned discreetly while the others were distracted by the game. The plane banked and gave them a birds-eye view of Mother Nature. A herd of giraffe of several hundred, were shooting by at what seemed to be just a few feet below the wheels of the plane.

Dacks realised his only salvation lay in a bar and permitted his mind the luxury of drifting back to the balmy perfection of the air conditioning to see Joseph drop two chunks of large ice into a long glass of English gin, fresh lime juice and soda water. His mind watched Joseph take a swizzle stick off the bar and stir his hoped-for drink.

Just as he imagined himself stretch out a hand for the desperately-needed drink, he was pressed violently back into his seat as the aircraft suddenly stood on its somewhat flimsy tail imitating a military aircraft in the art of vertical climb. The pilot's head swung from side to side and the eyes that turned to Dacks showed none of the alertness nor competence he expected from a pilot.

"Getting height... Getting height... Can you fly? Something trying... Passing out... Can't hold... Don't know."

Dacks's left foot moved up over and quickly in between those of the unconscious pilot and flicked the useless legs off the rudder bar. At the same time his right hand took hold of the half-wheel and pointed the aircraft out of the vertical to stop it stalling. The pilot's body fell against the farthest door but still prevented him from getting control of the screaming engine and falling aircraft.

"Herman, can you pull him over the top of his seat into your lap? He's passed out. I must get into his seat."

"Can you fly?"

"Not from this position."

"Give a hand, Anna. Now... Pull. Can you help free his legs, Mark? He's moving. Unhitch his arm, Anna. One, two, three, pull. And again. He can't go back any further. There isn't room this side."

"Hold him like that. I'll slip in between his legs."

The engine revs dropped and pressure on the left rudder brought the aircraft into straight flight. Dacks looked out of the window at the hard, dry bush a thousand feet below. The pilot had given him a chance. Pilots are made like that, he thought, though they don't pass out in the flying seat without a very good reason. He intended to find out.

"Pull him across. He can slump into my seat. Hello... Hello... Is that Falls control? This is Charlie Echo one seven four. No, this is not Danny Coetzee, it's Mark Dacks. Your friend has passed out on us in too confined a space. I'm flying Charlie Echo back to your airstrip and hope to land it in one piece in approximately seven minutes."

He banked the aircraft, steadied the compass on the course for the strip and glanced up sideways at the boot dangling some four inches away from his left eye.

He had the definite feeling that someone had just tried to kill him. For the first time he had an acute and terrible dislike for the pompous brain that had composed the letter delivered to his bedroom only yesterday. It was one thing to kill a selected enemy and quite another to make wholesale murder.

Against his will for vengeance he decided to get his guests out of Victoria Falls and make for the furthest point in their itinerary. This would take them to the east coast of Mozambique, in the Straits off Malagasy, where the main flow of his major business dealings culminated. The waters off the coast were little known and always dangerous. The sandbanks shifted on the ocean bottom and a safe channel for an ocean liner on Friday could shift so that it looked the same, but would founder an Arab dhow on the Monday. After more thought and a firmer control of his revenge, he decided not to mention any of this to his friend in the CID, who would be drinking with them in just over an hour. He realised an enquiry would be made but this could be left to the department of civil aviation.

The airstrip came into line. Almost absentmindedly he got permission to land.

He brought the small aircraft down and bounced the wheels on to the runway so the boot finally kicked him in the left eye. They settled more smoothly on to the strip and the speed went out with his pressure on the brakes. He stopped the plane short of the control tower and turned off the engine. He opened the pilot's door. He got one foot out of the aircraft and turned round so his back was out of the plane but his shoulders were inside and he was still facing the unconscious body, Herman Small and Anna Featherstone.

"Thanks, you two. Most others would have panicked. You were both incredible. I'd be grateful if you'd leave this bit out of your reports home, as pilots passing out isn't a frequent occurrence on Dacks's Tours. Now let's get him out and to hospital. He may be seriously ill."

9

CARA MIA

The black launch rode like a cork on the slight swell of the sea and was only kept in leash by the mooring rope that intermittently twanged and slackened as the sea and the *Cara Mia* exchanged brief, challenging words.

Dacks's captain was hunched at the other end of the small dinghy, boasting all of six inches freeboard, on its way out to the big launch. Gabe Saunders had his left hand on the tiller attached to the Seagull outboard motor that was phut-phutting its way and pushing the bows of the dinghy surprisingly easily over the ruffled sea.

Studying the fluted lines of the bows of his ship up ahead, Dacks was strongly satisfied. At speed, the water pushed in and under the hull and made the craft plane. The *Cara Mia* could travel at forty-two knots. The short-range radar sat fixed to the cockpit roof and the big, swaying aerials of the short radio transmitter and receiver pointed thinly at the morning sky of blue and dark patches of thunder cloud. It rained in Mozambique at that time of the year. When the deep-sea big game fishing launch was running among the marlin, the aerials looked like two more fishing rods, except that they didn't have lines with barracuda bait at the end, flicking the water while the fishermen watched and hoped for the big fish to come up and bite. With twin guns on the cockpit roof she would have looked more like a warship. The black of her steel body shone with the dull power of gun metal and the two 250-horsepower engines waited patiently below the waterline for the single touch of a commanding hand.

Gabe Saunders, the permanent captain, turned off the outboard motor of the dinghy, having judged that their speed was enough to bring them up to the big launch without pushing them past. They drifted in and Dacks gripped the flat, blunt stern and held the dinghy steady enough for Saunders to tie it up to the *Cara Mia*. Dacks leaned his weight on to his arms and pulled his body up without forcing down on the dinghy. He swung a leg over the side and trod the duck-boards that would let half an inch of water wash underneath them before the water was pushed out by a pump. The *Cara Mia* had every device for comfort.

He went up the two steps into the cockpit, followed by the captain, and seated himself on the high bar-type swivel stool in front of the wheel. With customary ease he checked the dials in front of him then fired the one engine, listened to its perfect roar with satisfaction, fired the second and listened intently to their joint power.

"You really look after these, Gabe."

"My job."

"They sound perfect. Pull up the anchor and we'll be on our way."

Dacks looked out of the Perspex windshield across the top of the foredeck at his friend pulling in the chain and finally the sea anchor. Gabe Saunders rolled with the boat as he came back, and went out of Dacks's sight. He was then heard to jump down on to the duck-boards in the well that was open to the heavens and held, when needed, the three paying fishermen who stood around the single fighting chair. The boat could only fight one big fish at a time and when a strike was made they got the lucky man quickly into the chair while the big fish took its first run. By the time the pressure was needed there, the big-game fisherman was tightly strapped in, with the butt of his rod in the cup in his wide leather belt. One, two, three hours later they let him out while the gaffs, wind and rope pulled in the sword-nosed fish. Then followed the beer drinking and line-shooting and consumption of total satisfaction in the big cabin with the large cocktail cabinet and adjacent fridge for cooling the beers and freezing the ice.

The *Cara Mia* had cost Dacks fifteen thousand pounds, though he never mentioned the figure as he didn't wish to excite the Inspector of Taxes in Salisbury. Most people believed the boat belonged to Gabe Saunders and this suited Dacks perfectly. The fees from the big-game fishermen in the season just paid for the upkeep and Gabe Saunders's salary. The fifteen thousand pounds investment was profitable in other ways that did not appear in the balance sheets of Safaris (Pvt) Limited.

Gabe Saunders knew the coast hundreds of miles in either direction as well as any man, and his African boatman, a very distant cousin of Joseph's, was just as skilled. Together, they operated the craft to Dacks's full satisfaction.

The engine revolutions drew to a climax and Dacks let the craft move forward. He swung the wheel and pointed the bows out to sea, then pulled on the power as much as it would take till the throttle was full and the launch had ceased to spray the windshield with sea water. The *Cara Mia* slowly rose up on the air being thrust under her hull and planed.

He brought the boat round in a wide curve and pointed her at the old Portuguese jetty on the mainland where Herman Small and Anna Featherstone were watching the craft's power with unrestrained excitement. Harold Ackit appreciated the lines and wished he had more time for such luxuries, then remembered the English weather and quickly forgot the idea. Francine Mure wondered if the boat was a phallic symbol, as it immediately reminded her of males that were strong. Mrs Hall wondered if the boat contained a bar, as she knew the island was over an hour's journey away. She thought of asking Korina Prague beside her, considered the improbability of Mark Dacks travelling the distance without being able to refresh himself with a gin sling, and discarded the idea, now certain in her mind of satisfaction on the water.

The boat grew larger as it came towards them, its bows sank on to the water, and the waves of sea sprayed out from its sides, catching the sun and the power of perfect line as Dacks eased off the throttle and handed the craft over to Gabe Saunders for mooring. The craft began to roll as the sea felt its buoyancy without the power of thrust and speed to counter and command.

Dacks went to the stern and waved a short-armed salute to his guests on the quay. They waved back across the short course of water that was growing less with the expert sideways motion caused by Gabe Saunders using the two engines in turn both forward and in reverse.

Dacks judged the distance and leapt across from the moving boat to the flight of stone steps that gave ease of disembarkation despite the height of the tide. His white shirt and dark blue jeans remained immaculate and were in no way spoiled by the sudden stretch.

He took a box of thirty First Lord from the breast pocket above the green motif of the shirt manufacturer and reached the top of the concrete steps two at a time in his rubber-soled shoes. He offered the smooth narcotic cylinders to Francine Mure and flicked her a light with his Ronson. He took one for himself, lit it and enjoyed the pure Rhodesian tobacco as it went down into his lungs with the fresh sea air from the Malagasy Straits.

The stern of the black launch eased itself to within six inches of the steps and held. Dacks helped the women into the boat. Herman Small tried to do it without assistance and was only prevented from cracking his skull by the sudden intervention of Dacks's iron arm. Harold Ackit came down the steps last and allowed himself to be expertly handed into the boat.

With the guests and luggage safely on board, Gabe Saunders took them out, carefully navigating a sand bar before opening up with both engines. The power and perfect marine engineering lifted the bows out of the water and streamed the *Cara Mia* across the green sea on top of three hundred fathoms of water, in search of the crescent island of Santa Salina set in its coral reef over the horizon.

The bar was opened immediately and went a long way towards relegating the previous three hour journey from Salisbury to nothing but memory. The present was again all-important.

Herman Small began to hope a tropical island would help him with his dirty little plans and allowed his eyes to rest hungrily on the tight little rear of Anna Featherstone as she leaned over the stern of the *Cara Mia*, her gin and lime on the gunwale beside her without as much as a ripple on its surface.

The thoughts of men were firmly in Anna's newly-awakened mind and she watched with a sense of expectant urgency the rushing sea going by beneath and away from her. She had some idea of the implications and possibilities of her thoughts and the further she rode away from the familiar and home, the less frightening became the prospect of delving into the new and yet oldest mystery of life and finding out whether the whole thing was as good as so many men had tried to tell her. She took her drink off the gunwale and turned round and rested both elbows on the gunwale behind her back.

She smiled at Herman as she raised the glass to her lips and immediately let loose a small flight of butterflies inside her stomach. The feeling was very pleasant and full of the future unknown. He raised his pint of Lion lager and drank, still keeping his eyes firmly on hers.

Dacks saw the exchange and imperceptibly raised his right eyebrow while mentally wishing them the best of luck. From the open door into the cabin, with the bar at the other end and the black cushioned seats running straight and then circling the bow so the point of the arrow was a half-full bottle of Plymouth gin, he watched Harold Ackit making another play for the sexual attentions of Korina Prague. Not for the first time, he admired the delicate smoothness with which she seemed to express a perfect sympathy with her subject and gave him the sensation of being alone in her thoughts and future affections. Dacks knew the tease would be manoeuvred until his plane took off for London but Harold Ackit would still think, right up to that moment, that if they happened to be on their own the limits would be taken to the end. To maintain the suspense, and to cut them off at the height of a new intimacy, he went down the three steps into the luxurious cabin and addressed Ackit.

"Would you like to throw a line over the side, Harold? Gabe brought some bait across with him. This stretch of water is said to be the second best marlin fishing in the world after Acapulco in Mexico. They still just hold the record over there but my bet is that it won't last for long. There's plenty of shark too, which give a good fight, as do the sailfish and barracuda."

"The biggest thing I ever caught was a mackerel."

"Try your luck. I'll get you out of trouble if it starts."

"Come on, Harold, I'll watch," said Korina. "I like to see a man catch a real fish."

"Said like that, how can I refuse?"

"Slow up on the speed, Gabe," Dacks called up to the captain, "we're going to fish."

The bows sank and the sky gave way to the horizon, and then just sea could be seen through the windshield over the bar. Korina went first up the three steps and was followed by Harold Ackit, determined to prove his youth against a fish.

Francine Mure watched Dacks follow them out and almost confided in Mrs Hall that she wished he would pay more attention to her. Instead she considered her pride and kept the remark to herself, concentrating on the second dry martini that Mrs Hall had poured for her out of the shaker that had been mixed by the target of her more specific needs. She was definitely growing frustrated, which was clearly marked by her second drink at tea-time. Sex in the afternoon had always been a different matter but drink time, for her, began at six.

Outside, with the sun scorching the fighting chair, the heat had driven Anna Featherstone and Herman Small into the cockpit next to Gabe Saunders, who was seated on the high swivel chair looking out of the windshield, while loosely holding the wheel at its correct compass bearing for the island. The craft had cut back to five knots. He was dressed in white shorts, white long socks, blue slip-on rubber-soled shoes and a white, impeccably laundered t-shirt that shouted out the name of the detergent manufacturer in its contrast to the deep, mahogany tan of four years of sailing up and down the Mozambique coast, and more specifically among the islands that had been consistently producing a most unusual financial crop for exactly the same forty-eight months.

Anna Featherstone was slowly but surely changing her mind about not liking older men as she found the masculinity of Dacks and Gabe Saunders overpowering.

Gabe Saunders had no preference for women. Given the circumstances, he found them perfectly acceptable in most shapes, sizes and ages provided they had that something which aroused the worst instincts in him. These instincts often rose, as many of the holidaying bachelor girls on the island had found to their cost and satisfaction on moonlit nights, when the pale fingers of the moon had just been able to slide in at the portholes of a gently rocking *Cara Mia* at rest on a smooth black sea.

The beauty for Gabe Saunders, and the fine record of reaching thirty-eight years of interesting age without getting married even once, was that these girls came from Salisbury and Johannesburg and stayed at the most for three weeks. And then off they went again to distant places and mail from the island was quite impossible as they had found out for themselves during their stay. Then another plane would come in and the eager, fresh faces of more female youth searched the island for an interesting male to produce a successful holiday. Having made his choice quickly from years of long experience, he always got an immediate response from an offer to sail in the *Cara Mia*. After that the romance of a fast launch and the sea, and as a last resort, the contents of the cocktail cabinet did all that was needed in an hour.

Unless instructed to by Dacks, he left Safaris's clients alone, since the other game they played with such success had to be planned and played with care. Spontaneous action was out unless danger called for it urgently. Yes, he thought to himself without the visible sign of a sigh, Anna Featherstone certainly had that something, and he forcibly stopped his mind from unhooking the small garment that was so firmly and yet softly holding in readiness two of the best-formed objects for his pleasure that he'd seen in twelve weeks. 'Very innocent,' he concluded, and this time he sighed like a Frenchman.

Dacks caught the sorrow in his friend's slow ejection of air, and, as he leaned across and took a heavy rod and a one-foot-diameter reel from the horizontal rack in front of the wheel, reminded him in Ndebele that there were more fish in the sea and that anyway a rest would do him good. Gabe Saunders winked in response and slightly increased the *Cara Mia*'s power to reach the correct speed for trolling.

Dacks went to the stern of the boat and pulled up a section of the duck-boarding. He then lifted the lid of a coolbox underneath and gripped the scaleless tail of a three-foot barracuda, pulling it out to reveal its long thin body and pointed head. The teeth in the long cavernous jaw were small and viciously sharp but the fish, fortunately, had been dead for two days and would only fool the big fish of the sea when it was trolled behind the launch.

Dacks thrust the big hook the size of a large man's hand down its throat and hooked right through so an inch of steel spike was showing from the gills.

"How's that, Harold? Just drop her over the side. That's it. Now press that release clip on the reel. Let her go further. Now you can hold it. The bait stays just below the surface at that distance of line and catches the sun at the same time. The marlin see that flash and come up for food. You don't often see them coasting on the surface. It's the same with the sharks. Now, clip the rod in there against the rail and we'll move out of the sun. A big strike will trip the ratchet and let the line run. You'll have time to get into the fighting chair and then the fun begins."

HAROLD ACKIT STOOD BACK under the shade of the cockpit's roof and allowed himself a brief smile. It had been so easy for him to get right into the Dacks's system and now he'd managed to gain his full confidence, which went as far as being taught how to fish for blue marlin.

It had taken his partner all of his trip with his girlfriend/assistant/mistress to realise that the leak was through the very man conducting his tour. In the first place, he had merely used the tour as a way of investigating Central and South East Africa and had only tumbled to the reality of Safaris Limited by chance when he'd gone for an evening stroll in the Wankie Game Reserve. He had got away from the rest huts to see, without being seen, an exchange of money for a pouch between Mark Dacks and an African. It was only then that the simplicity and ease of movement of their encounter came home to him. The Wankie Game Reserve had been the last stop before Salisbury Airport and flying back to London.

It hadn't taken his partner, Harold Ackit, more than twenty-four hours to uncover the connection between Mark Dacks and Korina Prague and subsequently the barman Joseph. As he hadn't wished to lose his opportunity on the tour, or his cover of legitimacy, it had been necessary to call upon the services of his agent in Rhodesia, who'd unfortunately proved himself unfit for the job. And then his luck had come and the tour had changed its itinerary.

He suspected, as he looked happily at his still-trolling line, that they were nearly at the main contact area where the authorities were notoriously lax. He watched his rod and again brought his mind back to thinking over the problem of how Mark Dacks got his stones into Europe and sold them. This was always the most difficult part of any such operation that wished to avoid both customs dues and income tax. This he knew very well from the experience of his own organisation. Ackit knew that if he could find the outlet he would be able to stop the operation completely, and ensure that no one else would be able to keep Dacks's system going, after Dacks had been dealt with by himself, once and finally for all.

They should have known that the man would be able to fly a plane. They still knew very little about the man's background despite Ackit's own careful probing. So far they knew about his tour business and the fact that it didn't make the right kind of profit and yet Mark Dacks was never short of money. They knew that he was a third generation Rhodesian, which probably accounted for his ease of movement around Africa. Familiarity with, and a deep mutual trust between Dacks and the African people, would give him the many contacts he needed to move the amount of glitter he appeared to be getting out. It obviously helped in that part of the world, thought Harold Ackit, to be able to speak so many languages. Having heard him jabber away to Gabe Saunders in a tongue that sounded as if the speaker was going to click up his tonsils, he was convinced that the captain of the *Cara Mia* was part of the organisation as well and that the *Cara Mia* was one of the main props in the lesser-known part of the business.

He mentally noted all of this to pass on to his agent in Beira at eight-fifteen that night, his regular transmission time. His short-wave receiver/transmitter looked like any other innocent transistor receiver of the type that patrolled the beaches of the world in the idle hands of teenagers. From Beira, London would be informed by a more powerful unit. With each change of location, Ackit had become more fully aware of the size of Dacks's organisation and had realised that only a small portion of the stones came from the known mines in the way that their own supplies reached Europe. He wondered where the rest originated from.

He thought of his wife and his stupid, petty family problems and wondered if, over the past twenty-five years, she had ever had the glimmer of an idea of where all the money she spent really came from. The word 'banking' went through his mind and made him laugh almost out loud at the ridiculously small profit they actually made out of the apparently major part of their interests.

He looked at Mark Dacks just in front of him, calmly studying the sea beyond the rigid line and rod, and conjectured at what a surprise he would get if he knew what was coursing through his guest's mind, a man he no doubt thought to be another rich and stupid tourist under the spell of the masterful charm of Mark Dacks. Then, noticing the deep lines of concentration on Dacks's forehead, he wished he had the ability to read his adversary's mind.

Yes, his partner had also been right in saying that the man was extraordinary and that he had an unusual way of life that could well be emulated if one had that turn of mind. But Harold Ackit had made it his business to have always the turn of mind that was most suited to increasing the wealth in his private bank account in Switzerland. He believed in money like a religion, though he often talked against it in public and during the time of the betrayal he had even managed to make himself think differently. There had always been that element of Jekyll and Hyde in his make-up and the complete change of personality for his public life had ensured that the minds of the police had not, to the best of his very good knowledge, been turned against him. He and his company were thought of well enough in the highest circles, as well as in the lowest, the latter of which included the occasional policeman sent along to snoop in the course of routine. The front he'd kept up over twenty-five years had been both material and psychological, hence its unrelenting success.

His mind focused on a dorsal fin coming at great speed towards the bait. With a vicious 'tung' the head of the rod ducked, the ratchet gave way and the reel hummed as the line shrieked away from the *Cara Mia*.

"Grab the line. You've got a shark."

Accepting Mark Dacks's urgent instructions, he rapidly moved out of the shade and lunged for the bent double rod, gripped it strongly and lifted it out of the iron hoop. The reel revolved like a tortured Catherine wheel. He got himself and the rod into the fighting chair by letting the big fish, with the three-foot barracuda stud in its throat, have its way. With difficulty, he got the butt of the rod into the cup hanging from his deep-sea fishing belt. Mark Dacks pulled the straps on the fighting chair into place for him over his chest and thighs and rod. He put his feet on the wooden bar in front and got a good purchase for his legs.

"Put some drag on the reel. Make it hard for him. More than half your line's out already."

He again obeyed instructions and put some thumb pressure on the indicated drag and felt the pressure build up in his back and leg muscles. The fish felt immensely strong.

"Give it a hard jerk. He may have the hook in his belly. That way you can pull up enough of his guts to suffocate him in his own innards."

The heavy line responded to his now desperate jerk and the hook held. The line went on out at an increased speed that tautened every muscle in his body to such a pitch of agony that he began to wonder, as he was forced to let the straps hold him to the chair and the *Cara Mia*, whether Mark Dacks knew exactly who he was and was using the shark as a means of torture. His eyes focused on the straps and he realised with fear that they were buckled behind him along with the one that had interlaced the rod. He couldn't let go and free himself if he tried. He had always imagined from books that the rod was left free. Fear came out in the beads of cold sweat that began to appear on his forehead. And the sweat was sucked up by the searing power of the tropical sun.

"Jerk it again and plug the drag."

With the desperation of a dying man he jabbed the drag in flush with the reel and thrust himself backwards. His face jerked up at the sky and then snapped back on to his chest with a flip that tore at his neck muscles.

"You've got him, Harold."

The voice of Korina Prague injected the last ounce of energy into him and he pulled back again.

"Now reel him in. He'll come with you some of the way."

Mark Dacks's voice was like the torturer's whip, but he obeyed in the hope of finding salvation. He knew he couldn't find it by himself as his mind was unable to think of anything but pain, and, anyway, shark fishing had never been part of his training as a banker or trader in stolen gems.

Surprisingly, the big fish let itself be wound in with the line. This gave him sufficient confidence to look up and along the progressively shortening line that was as taut as piano wire, to the end where the huge fish wallowed. The shark grew bigger and bigger as it was drawn towards the boat by the mechanical turn of his arm. Fear for its size rode up from his intestines.

Apart from the fin riding over to one side the monster looked nothing like a shark. It pushed its ugly head up from the water and showed the line going in past the double row of teeth for over two feet of jaw. Its head was flat above the mouth and supported two wings like squashed flat dumbbells, that glistened at the tip of each side, with an eye that let the fish search back past its own fat belly to see through three hundred and sixty degrees. The eyes were the size of well-boiled prunes and they watched Harold Ackit with a fixed dead stare.

"You got him, Harold. Just keep winding. The hammerhead shark is the easiest to kill that way and the most difficult to land if you don't. That fish should weigh five hundred pounds. The record in this stretch of sea is seven hundred and fifty-three so you didn't catch a big one. Just reel him in. Hey, Gabe, come and give us a hand. Do you feel strong, Herman? Grab that gaff and the rope. If we don't get him out of the water one of his friends will come in for a meal and once the blood is spilt there'll be thirty or forty of his cousins at his funeral."

Mark Dacks sent the first barbed hook of a steel gaff into the shark's side and, using all of his strength, pulled the grey slimy shark in parallel to the side of the drifting launch. With the engines turned off there was no chance of foul-hooking the twin screws. With expert ease, Gabe Saunders looped a rope over the slanted tail with the small dissymmetrical fin underneath that would prevent the rope slipping off.

"Herman, stick your gaff in its shoulder. Right, now, give me that rope."

The second noose slid over the hammerhead and drew tight. Mark Dacks put his rope on a pulley nearest to his straight pull at right angles from the fish and in line with the shark's head, and Gabe Saunders did the same for the tail. There were pulley wheels at two-foot intervals along the stern sides. Together they evenly winched the floppy fish out of the sea. It rose tug by tug without getting so much as a glance from Harold Ackit, who lay back in the fighting chair with his body wrenched in every part from the power of the big fish. First the dorsal fin was jerked clear of the side and then some of the back came over. They tied their taut ropes to the opposite side of the launch.

Mark Dacks went back and gripped the handle of his gaff that was still stuck in the fish and Gabe Saunders sank in another just short of the tail. The three men heaved in and rolled the fish over the gunwale and dropped it into the boat. Its body was too big to lie straight. The dead, open eyes watched them with reproach and surprise. Some blood from the gaffs had dripped into the water and three fins circled some ten yards off from the launch.

Gabe Saunders went back to the controls. The engines turned. The *Cara Mia* swung round on to its heading for Santa Salina and power ran along the length of the boat lifting its bows out of the water. They streamed away from the three sharks, their food snatched out of their mouths, still puzzling the smell of blood.

Twenty minutes later the first smudge of the island appeared out of the sea with the sun behind. The stretch of sea in between came up and went under the bows of the *Cara Mia*. Palm trees grew out of the smudge that became a crescent island with brightly coloured, two-storied houses in among the palms almost to the water's edge.

As they drew closer to the cluster of deep-sea, big-game fishing boats riding at anchor in the bay, people could be seen sitting on the slope of the beach, while others were swimming in the sea away from the white sand, made exclusively from ground seashells and coral. One of the fishing boats was flying the black flag of a marlin catch. Punts were being poled to and from the boats stacked high with the catch, fishermen and empty beer bottles. The Africans standing on the wooden lips at the back of the punts leaned gracefully back on their twelve-foot poles till the tips were left just above the surface and then they pulled up, more and more, and the thin poles grew up above the Africans only to go down again to seek the sandy bottom and purchase for the push once more.

The sun behind the island threw the palm trees into silhouette with their long trunks curving at all angles to the dust-blue sky.

Gabe Saunders turned the black, powerful bows of the *Cara Mia* towards the gap in the coral reef that was only navigable at high tide; some thirty yards to either side of where they went through at two knots, the coral would have torn the steel of the hull into shreds.

Inside, the floor of the bay was a muddy sand where the sea flowers hid the more venturesome tropical fish that had swum in with the tide from beyond the reef. A similar small boat to the one used from the mainland put out from beside the small jetty with Yasani, Gabe Saunders's number two, bent comfortably over the Seagull outboard motor. From the launch, the freeboard of the dinghy seemed almost too little to let the small craft float.

Mark Dacks dropped the land anchor over the side and the chain ran out till the heavy iron touched bottom. Gabe Saunders took them away until the point of the anchor dug deep into the seabed. He shut off the German engines and the lap of water was heard against the hull. The smell of the seashore was strong.

Harold Ackit looked at his fish with an awakening pride, as some of the pain had gone out of his back. The cold Laurentina lager given to him by Mark Dacks had finally relieved his suspicions of being found out, especially as the benefactor had explained that he always strapped the rod to the beginners as he had lost too much tackle from panic in the past. Harold Ackit disliked the look of friendly understanding being bestowed upon him by a beer-drinking Gabe Saunders. He had never liked the successful athletic types. He again studied the island and was surprised by the number of tourists watching the boat come in, the island looked too small for so many people.

A small launch followed Yasani's dinghy. A short, square-shouldered man was hunched in the cockpit. He looked, getting nearer, like a gorilla. He was very dark with a square head above powerful shoulders that were both thick and wide. Without the smiling, clear blue eyes in the mahogany face he would have frightened even an innocent man.

Diogo de Almeida brought the island's launch alongside the *Cara Mia* on the other side to Yasani. The big face broke into a smile for Mark Dacks – a row of pure white, very even teeth making themselves known to everyone in turn. Francine Mure reflected that there would be a wealth of pleasure in such a face, and Mrs Hall, having gathered that this big, very dark man with the curly hair was the owner of the island, concluded that he didn't look the type to let his hotel run out of liquor.

Diogo de Almeida had been running Santa Salina as a tourist hotel and big-game fishing centre for twelve years and, though he had sometimes run out of the more obscure brands of alcohol, he had never run out of the hard tack, the wine or the beer. With agility surprising to the watchers new to his feats, he jumped up into the *Cara Mia* with a rope in one hand. Mark Dacks took the rope and handed him a cold beer, then tied up the small launch.

Yasani just got his back away from the descending hand of Mark Dacks before setting-to to get the dead shark into the shark-free bay for towing to the shore. His family had been closely associated with Dacks's for fifty years and he had had considerable practice at avoiding that crippling, traditional backslap.

Mark Dacks introduced the owner of the island to his guests and Francine Mure was not disappointed by the strong, sun-tanned hand that shook her very much smaller white one.

Harold Ackit tried to meet the man's gaze with a friendly acknowledgement but almost physically recoiled from the depth of power lying in the back of those blue eyes. Instinctively he feared the man and then wondered why. Running his organisation had not always brought him into contact with the nicest of people. The power of the Portuguese man in front of him was not only to be found in the size of his shoulders, he thought.

It needed very little mental agility for Harold Ackit to realise that the Portuguese was another member of the organisation that had defied his own for too many years. The island was Mark Dacks territory, where the law was Diogo de Almeida. With the real law some two hundred miles away by sea in Beira, Ackit decided that it was an ideal place for him to complete his plans, but first he needed a little reinforcement and a boat as fast as the *Cara Mia*.

10

HIDE AND SEEK

The skin-tight jeans pronounced each curve of Korina Prague's body from her hips down to her ankles. Every man in the bar surreptitiously glanced down to just below her waist level as she walked past a young man wearing equally tight black jeans and plucking a Portuguese guitar.

She continued on her way towards the bar and towards Mark Dacks seated comfortably on a bar stool. In front of a vast pile of piri-piri crab claws that he was methodically working his way through from left to right. The white silk of her blouse did nothing to hide a blue bra that, with an extension of its material, covered to just above her navel.

Dacks passed the plate of piri-piri crab across to her as she sat down on the stool he'd been keeping vacant for her next to his.

The barman finished mixing the lime gin sling he'd started when he'd first seen her coming through the door and placed it carefully on the highly polished mahogany bar in front of her. She lifted it up and took a sip, while at the same time sending him a thanks with her eyes over the rim of the long glass. She put down the glass and stretched a well manicured hand towards the oval plate of crabs' legs and selected herself a claw that had particularly white-looking meat. Methodically she began to feed the flakes of sweet crab from the shell into her mouth past her pink-shaded, very inviting lips. She caught Mark Dacks watching her and felt her stomach, that should have known better, flip over. His tan contrasted too strikingly with his white yachting shirt to enable her to maintain a normal equilibrium. She licked some of the piri-piri from her lips in self-defence and returned her attention to emptying her particular shell of crab meat. The guitar music was plaintive and a little too romantic to enable all of her attention to go back to the food, however.

"Glad to be back on the island?" Dacks asked.

"Yes. It has memories, if you remember."

"How can I forget? Outside Rhodesia, it's my favourite place in the world."

"I feel relaxed and safe here somehow. Diogo has such a firm control of everything. I don't have any worries on his island."

"He's a great man to have on our side, even if he's been in love with you for the past three years."

"I think we should come here every trip."

"I'm sure he thinks the same but we wouldn't be offering the best to our clients if we brought them here out of the big-game fishing season."

"Why didn't you tell me about the plane?"

"By the time I brought her down at the airport it was over and finished. How did you find out?"

"Your old school friend in the CID let it slip."

"He's less of a fool than he lets people believe. He was no good at bookwork at school but his IQ was never at fault, and some of the pranks he dreamed up were quite marvellous."

"Can we get out on the boat by ourselves tonight?"

"At the moment, I can see no reason why not. We can go across to the big island if I can still remember my way past the reefs."

"I don't think you'll forget."

"No, you're right. Forgetting that kind of information is dangerous. Drink up and join me with another sling. That damn piri-piri is designed to make us drink, not that I need too much encouragement."

The sword of a blue marlin pointed directly down from the wall at his glass as he raised it to get the barman's attention. An entire sail-fish was trying to swim along the wall above the bottles of alcohol a little further to the left, but it had been trying to do this trick for seven years and had never moved.

The barman took his glass as Anna Featherstone came up to the bar behind him in another costume entirely and successfully designed to titillate the senses of the male sex. Herman Small followed in a pair of shorts and shirt that clearly showed that he was more at home in such attire than he was in an evening suit. Mark Dacks ordered him a cold Laurentina without being asked, a brown sherry for Anna and then caught sight of Mrs Hall and added a dry martini to his order with one part Noilly Prat to ten parts Booths gin.

The bar filled up around them with the talk of the big-game fisherman. They were all loud in their own certain determination that they would be flying the black flag of the marlin catch the next day. The air was cooled by overhead fans that circulated the hot, salt air that came in from the Indian Ocean some few feet outside and some more feet down below the long, castle-type windows that would have taken a circle of bowmen shoulder to shoulder, if the need had ever arisen. The sea outside was silent and pushed softly around the coral rocks on its way inshore with the tide. The guitar played to the night, separated from the people and almost even from the Portuguese musician who was plucking the haunting strings in turn and tune.

The room kept hold of the sophisticated people cut off from their world and sustained only by the memory of their society which told them to behave as usual. This became less and less necessary as the days passed and the tide of mankind was left behind. The result was informal sophistication that only needed the bare essentials of clothes to let the rest of the body wash in the warm balm of the tropical nights. The contrast to normal life was greatly felt and enjoyed all the more because of the difference. There was a natural power that covered everything and everyone on the island and made the instincts of people seem normal. A philosophy that had been the undoing of more than one girl in her search for romance by the side of the coral sea. They never forgot that first time, even as old people, because in the setting of Santa Salina nothing was sordid and the acts left memories that were good and full of burning nostalgia. People had found for a few weeks by the white sands, with coral reefs rainbowed in the midday sun, with the coconuts for the taking from the top of long trunks with feet marks cut at intervals right up to the palm fronds and waiting to be climbed, with the soft clean balm of the Indian Ocean and men like Mark Dacks, Gabe Saunders and, for the more adventurous and brave, Diogo de Almeida, a rare perfection never felt by some people in the world but always within reach of the lovers who came to the pearl of the Indian sea. In two or three days they all fell under the spell and from then the days went by without time or pain, everything – sleeping, waking – a thing of happiness and pleasure.

It had happened to Mark Dacks and Korina Prague. Each time they returned and walked out alone on the crescent island, or took the boat out to sea for a landfall away from the world, the feeling returned and they were again young people, no cares, no wants, no worries. Plunging back into their business afterwards was all the more exciting for the interlude, and when the time came round again they went back into pure romance for a few hours, sometimes days, and their world was then only themselves.

Diogo de Almeida walked briskly into the bar and across to Mark Dacks. An open charcoal-grey shirt fell outside his long white trousers and the white calf shoes on his feet were not surprising. His eyes took in Korina Prague with an unhappy acceptance of fate, speculated on the younger one's figure only to establish her age as being less than twenty, which was a pity. He only embarked on adventures with women over twenty-five as he had no intention of marrying before the age of forty-five and girls of reasonable maturity were more sensible about that sort of thing.

He waited for the conversation between Dacks and Anna Featherstone to stop for a moment and then tapped his friend on the shoulder.

"Can I see you for ten minutes?"

"Of course, Diogo. Will you all excuse me for a few moments? Korina will look after you. Put the drinks on my chits and I'll sign them when I get back. Francine Mure and Harold Ackit should be along soon. Dinner is at nine-thirty in the continental style. Don't eat too much of the crab or else you won't enjoy the real seafood that Senhor de Almeida always provides straight from the sea via his kitchens."

He followed the broad shoulders out of the bar with the smallest element of unease in his mind; his friend usually waited until he was alone and away from his guests before taking him aside to talk business.

Outside, they went down a flight of marble stairs curving down to a patio built out over the coral rocks with the sea lapping its feet. The marble had proved to be the most expensive shipment in the building costs but it had added a brilliant display of luxury and flamboyance. As they walked down, the marble reflected the strong light of the moon and the stars glittered in its surface. Dacks followed Diogo away from the terrace down another narrow flight of steps that had been cut into the coral then smoothed to eliminate the jagged edges.

His feet felt the soft smoothness of the crushed coral and seashell sand.

His puzzlement increased as they walked out around the head that jutted from the east side of the island. They moved into the main coconut grove and past the pockets of orchids that had been planted into the trunks of the palms. The palms grew straight from the sand. The path was patterned by the moon shadows of the straw-hatted palms with the feathery fronds unmoving in the still sea air.

The buildings and lights receded behind them and all that was suggestive of man's presence finally was the clank of the turning wheel on a distant well sucking fresh water out of a deep hole in the sand. They moved quietly as if by instinct beneath the palms. Dacks looked up at the angled trunk of the tallest of them; its coconuts were silhouetted by the brilliant white of the moon beyond. The sky-smoothed fronds were spread out in giant protective arms from the growing centre of the nuts at the topmost height of the crescent trunk.

Diogo signalled him to get low to the ground, and they crept slowly from tree to tree, expertly walking up the moon-flung shadows of the coconut palms. Dacks strained to see through the grove and flexed his hands in readiness. He stopped abruptly. The air, some fifty yards up through the palm trees, was crackling with the static and distorted words of a short-wave radio receiver. Dacks strained to form the noise into words but without success. The noise shut out as quickly as it had come and was replaced by the soft monotone of a man's voice that was free of static, indicating that it was being heard on Santa Salina by the naked ear. Again, however, the softly spoken words were unintelligible.

Dacks moved silently and swiftly forward, listening as he moved. A hard, metallic click stopped him again and the flesh crawled on his chest and spine. He saw movement between the trees and briefly the shape of a man's shoulders with his head bent forward. He and Diogo quickened their pace but a sand dune came between them and the radio operator. With nothing to hide behind but sand, they broke into a run through the silent coconut palms. They slowed up as they topped the dune. To one side was the sea with the moon spangling the slight ripples. To the other side was the path leading up into the chalets that were lightless and silent. There was no sign of a man or of any movement. Dacks searched the sea with his eyes right out to the horizon but there were no boats either to swim to nor talk to with a short-range transmitter.

They moved up towards the path. They climbed up it together and quickly walked along past the fronts of the chalets staring darkly through the palms towards the glint of the moon-bathed, silent sea.

The concrete path led them to the steps that went up to the marble terrace, from where it was possible to pass on into the public rooms of the hotel. They went inside the building and along a corridor panelled with dark wood that gave off a rich, musty smell. The night always drew this scent. They turned off into the last room, Diogo's office. Diogo closed the door behind them and switched on the powerful overhead light. There was one black, heavy desk in the centre of the room and a rush mat in front of its lion-clawed feet on the dark mukwa-block floor. The desk was as highly polished as the bar upstairs. Behind it, through the long, archer windows, the sea glinted under the moon, the waves just visible against the inside glare of the electric light.

Diogo de Almeida seated himself behind the desk in his high-armed wooden chair with its crude and powerful carvings on the arms and the tall, pointed back, like the Confessor's chair except that this one had been created by Africans with the symbols of pagan power as their motive force. The effect was crude and powerful. There was a trace of Arab thinking in the snakes, lending the use of their bodies for the chair's arms, but the lions roaring at the ends were all African.

Dacks moved a cane chair from the corner of the room beside the waist-high copper urn, by the simple expedience of lifting it in his right hand and putting it down again some fifteen paces further away in front of the writing table of massive proportions. Dacks sat himself down. The lion-headed snakes seemed to watch him carefully. He raised his eyes and looked straight at his friend. Momentarily, he raised both eyebrows in a question mark.

"I hoped you'd see who it was as well but that didn't matter so much as you hearing that transistor set. I know the communications I permit the public on the island are a little slow and that it's often quicker to post a letter after leaving the island, but it doesn't explain someone radioing behind my back who is meant to have nothing in mind but a holiday. And, what's more, Mark, it was one of your guests."

One dark eyebrow rose and formed another question.

"I don't know his name, and there again I didn't go up and shake his hand in broad daylight to get the best of looks, but I'm pretty certain it was that guy who caught the shark on the *Cara Mia* this afternoon."

"What would Harold Ackit want to stand out on a deserted beach and prattle into a radio transmitter for?"

"That's the big question. Keep an eye on him. I'll have Yasani go through his clothes to see what can be found."

"Funny, his partner came on the trip last year. They're big commercial bankers in Lombard Street but he's told me more than once that he doesn't wish to think of business on the trip, let alone hear about it. Sure, make a search. He must have something to hide with a set like that, and even if he is harmless I'd like to know who he was talking to from the beach just now."

Diogo de Almeida leaned forward and pulled open the small cupboard on the right of his desk, clicked open the hidden door of the refrigerator and took out a crystal decanter of white wine, which he placed on its waiting stand on top of his desk. With two quick movements he closed both the doors and opened the corresponding door on the other side and drew out two long-stemmed, elegantly bowled and lipped, minutely thin-glassed glasses. He placed them on the highly-polished table with one hand and closed the well-made door with the other. He removed the heavy glass stopper from the decanter and without apparent effort lifted the wine decanter to the nearest glass and poured, cut back, moved it across, and poured into the second glass. The cold, yellow wine frosted the glasses outside and the harsh electric light made liquid patterns through the glass.

Dacks accepted the proffered glass and raised it towards his friend before bringing it across to his mouth and taking a long pull of the dry full-bodied wine that cooled for that moment the whole of his body.

"Where has the pick-up been arranged and when, Diogo?"

"Tomorrow night. It's been said you must bring a lot of money as the pile of stones now on the island of Bagota is very high and very wide. There will be much celebrating, so they say, when the transfer takes place. Many people from many places are on the island now. They are the top collectors who know your business and have sworn to keep silent. They say many of the stones have come from a newly-found diamond deposit near Sofala. I have heard that the stones are very good, but are becoming more difficult to find as the diggers are now many feet below the surface, and the face of the big hole crumbles when it rains so that it has to be dug out again with spades. It is difficult to get the earth out. Only ten people can work in the hole at the same time. One of the tribe worked in a mine at Kimberley and has told them about conveyor belts and mechanical grabs. They're going to ask you tomorrow to spend some of their money on this machinery and to bring it to Sofala for them."

"Mine machinery is heavy stuff and if we start shifting it in large quantities the authorities will soon realise someone's found something and will want to know who and where."

"Can't you find an area in Rhodesia that isn't an exclusive prospecting area and stake a diamond claim?"

"I'd have the Mines Department snooping and taking samples and the income tax people wanting to see my books. If this salting had been possible we'd have done it instead of smuggling. To operate in an environment protection zone you have to do it unnoticed. And then again if I said I'd found diamonds in a free area they'd make me sell through the central selling organisation, as I couldn't sell legally in quantities elsewhere. And in most places the rock history would show to the Mines Department that I was crazy to think diamonds were there at all. All the likely places have an EPA slapped on them already. The big corporations can afford to spend the required millions on prospecting in their EPAs and government knows it's the only way to get an intensive search. It's a vicious circle that only the very rich and Mark Dacks can win."

"What are you thinking?"

"We'll have to smuggle through the equipment in pieces and make the pieces look as though they're meant for something else. We can take them to our side of the Zambezi by Land Rover and have trucks waiting on the other side, upstream some fifty miles from Sofala. It'll need a lot of organisation but there are only a few police and the Game Department in that part of the country. The tsetse fly have seen to that; not a good place to spend any length of time in. I'll talk to them at Bagota and find out what kind of soil and rocks surround the deposit and whether there's water nearby. With plenty of water, sorting the loose rock and soil is easy as the diamonds sink to a certain level and stick on a belt coated with an oil slime that holds the stones. They'll find many thousands more diamonds that way. Thanks, I'll have another. The wine you keep in your blasted desk is the best on the island."

"Of course."

"And you always have it decanted so no one knows the name of the vineyard."

"Of course. You think I'm crazy enough to tell everyone? When no one knows about a good wine it stays cheap."

"You should have collected enough at two and half per cent of sales not to worry about the price."

"So I have, Mark, but having created the mystery wine I like to keep it that way. Shall we go and join the ladies upstairs? We have been away half an hour. I want to look again at this Harold Ackit and then there is also Korina."

"Yes, you are right... There is Korina."

"Delightful."

"Here again, we agree."

"I know... And here is the pity... Such a waste for the girl. *Saúde*. I will tell you the name of my wine in my will."

"Most kind of you."

"Always a friend. Even when dead."

"I will leave you Korina in mine."

"Not, I'm afraid, a fair exchange, Mark. She is even much better than my wine."

"From you, Diogo, that is the greatest compliment. After you, Don Juan."

11

THE DEEP BLUE SEA

Mark Dacks propped his elbows on the smooth white sand, put his square-cut chin into the palms of his hands, dug his bare toes behind him into the hot sand to find the cooler moisture underneath and looked out to sea over the searing reflection of the ten o'clock sun.

The palm tree above him swayed in the morning breeze and the uniform line of tassels along each side of the crescent wands rustled gently and gave an illusion of coolness. The sharp shadows playing on Dacks's shoulders rippled the sun but the depth of his tan was so rich that it wouldn't go any darker. The tan was a good contrast to the white sand and large white towel underneath him.

His eyes swivelled gently away from the sea, and the one snorkel furrowing the blue ocean some thirty yards off shore, and contemplated a tall girl in a black lace bathing costume that left little to the imagination from a distance. A two-inch black circular felt band went smoothly around her long white throat and similar smaller bands were secured around her ankles. Her sandals were held on by leather thongs. The thongs were studded with the rich red, green and opal-coloured stones of the East. Around her hips, and held up by the firm and inviting curves of her perfect body, was a chain of fine gold that let one end pass through an elaborate black padlock in filigree imitation iron and dangled invitingly in line with the central juncture of her long, curved, fishnet-stockinged legs.

She carried a glass tray with three yellow pineapples on top. She was the latest inspired idea of Diogo de Almeida's, all of which, when added together, had made his hotel more than pay. His latest invention also happened to provide a changing pattern for his evening life. The girls flocked to the agency in Salisbury which employed them and sent them out for three weeks at a time. The young ladies achieved a holiday for nothing and, depending on their charms, either got some good exercise or a fortune. They enjoyed themselves, as there was no rule about sitting with the guests either in the day or at night.

This one had a manner that attracted Dacks more than usual. He kept his gaze directly on her sunglasses and sensed she was looking directly into the thoughts behind his eyes.

The top of the pineapples had been sliced away, allowing a silver spoon to jut from each fruit and glint in the sunlight. She stopped a yard short in front of him so that he was only able to study her well-formed, firm feet and the delightful turn of her ankles. As she bent with the tray held down to him, he could smell the young musk of an inviting perfume. He wrinkled his nostrils in appreciation. She took one of the pineapples on its glass plate from the tray and put it down on the white towel in front of him and gave him, as additional comfort, an even more delightful view of those few inches of normally hidden flesh that propriety said he shouldn't have been able to see on a beach, even the beach of Santa Salina, when the two concerned were not alone. He placed the index finger of his right hand on the imitation ruby just above her big toe and pressed. She stood up and released another wave of the very inviting musk, and his finger slipped on to her skin.

"Go and give the couple over there your other two pineapples and then come back and tell me your name."

He let his finger move off the smooth white skin and, instead of turning to the fruit, allowed himself the pleasure of watching her rear move away from him. It rose and fell in the jerked, caressing movements of a most sex-inviting walk. His more barbarous instinct rose to the fore as she bent down with her back to him and, with her legs straight, placed the two large fruits in front of first Anna Featherstone, who greeted it with glee, and then Herman Small. Herman was not so enthusiastic about the pineapple, as he too had been distracted from the plate to the same few inches of well-moulded, smooth and most inviting flesh that had had so much written about its sins.

Dacks stretched for a First Lord that he took out by fumbling inside the packet. He lit it by instinct without once taking his eyes off the girl who was again walking towards him. With the cigarette in his mouth, he rolled on to his back, held his left elbow propped behind him and patted the clean expanse of his towel with his right hand.

She put down the tray and knelt on the towel, sinking an inch into the sand beneath, then sat down beside him, stretching her long legs out parallel to Dacks's. He considered them again at leisure as he offered her a First Lord from the box. He lit her cigarette and decided that her legs were perfect. The eyes he looked into as she hooked her heavy dark glasses off her nose were green.

"I'm Mark Dacks."

"Yes… I know. I'm called Anna-Marie, which is quite enough really. I mean one doesn't need all the other names. What are those things?"

"Snorkels and masks. I always bring an extra pair in case I meet someone like you and then I can watch for the fish in good company. That thing there is a spear gun. Have you looked at the fish?"

"No, I only got here last night. It is beautiful, you can say."

"It is a jewel among islands."

"The sand is so white and the sea is so blue."

"And the fish are every colour of the rainbow. Many of them have been given the names of game, birds and fish. Out there, just down under the blue surface, are the big, twenty-pound parrot fish with beaks just like the birds and bodies that are fat and pale translucent-blue with yellow and emerald green stripes. Then there are the zebra fish in black stripes as well as orange. There are the good eating fish like the sea bream. There are grouper down in the deeper water, big ugly fish with heavy flake meat that is perfect when cooked in the French herbs. There is the coral in all its colours and growing shapes, and the walking shell fish. It has been said that just out there and further is the most exciting sea in the world. The sword-nosed marlin come in close to the reef. Further out are the sharks, the ragged-tooth, the sand shark, the tiger and the grey shark. It is an exciting sea. Come, I'll take you out."

"What about the sharks?"

"Not even the non-human variety will touch so beautiful a body. And if they try to get fresh I will discourage them. The water is so clear and there is all the time to take action, unlike the waters of the Zambezi where I learned to use that gun's great-grandfather. In the day, the island is here for the sea, and later when the sun goes down, it is here for other things. Santa Salina... What better than that for a name and a place? Just look at it all around us. It is the only place I have found in the world that is entirely made for pleasure."

"I think maybe you love this island."

"I think maybe you are right, Anna-Marie... Pure paradise. Yes, a name to roll on the tongue and savour like Santa Salina. Will you have some of the pineapple you brought me first? Diogo has them made specially for me. See, try this mouthful and you will taste the wild cherries of the Kirsch liqueur. Yes, this one is good. You agree?"

"Perfect."

"They make this by chunking out the hard centre, slicing free the fruit inside and cutting it into pieces before putting it back with the Kirsch poured over it afterwards. The whole is then left in the bottom of a refrigerator for half a day. Try some more. You don't mind my spoon if I don't mind yours."

"No, I don't mind your spoon. It makes so little difference really."

"Like the name?"

"Oh no, the name is important. It gives an expression of sound to the character inside the person."

"Have another mouthful of this 'Kirschilated' pineapple and tell me where you were born to have such a fascinating accent."

"I am from Vienna... You know, where they did all those waltzes before my grandmother was born."

"What made you come to Africa?"

"What is it that made *you* come to Africa? Maybe it is the same."

"I don't think so, Anna-Marie. What a name, and all the way from Vienna together with eyes like an emerald pool. No, Mark Dacks was here to start with. I was born under a mopane tree."

"And your father?"

"I think he was born beside a baobab."

"I have seen their pictures. They have very big girths and no branches. I was in England for some time where I learnt to speak English but since I have come to Rhodesia I haven't seen so much of the country as I would like."

"You should try a Dacks tour."

"They are saying it costs a thousand pounds. No, it is easier this way and costs me nothing, and if I am careful I shall be all right."

"Are you being careful now?"

"Now doesn't matter, as the sun is shining."

"Have another mouthful. It's still cold. Then I will show you the sea."

"I can't swim in this costume."

"Take off the bands around your neck and ankles and your sandals. Ah, yes, now I see. Your beauty, with that long, long neck, is better uncluttered. I have flippers for you too. I think I can see a good suntan lotion over there beside Herman. It is good just now in the morning. An hour from now and the sun will be too hot for you. Herman! Throw me Anna's tube of lotion. I have a customer."

The 'Sea and Ski' sailed elegantly in its tube, turning over and over in its trajectory, and landed firmly some thirty yards away from Herman Small in Dacks's outstretched right hand.

"Herman, do you play cricket?"

"Yes."

"That was a damn good throw."

"Makes catching easy."

Dacks winced, rubbed the end of his right elbow, and returned his concentration to the woman seated on his towel in front of him. He turned Anna-Marie around to face the coconut palm and exposed the delightful plunge of her bare back. He squeezed some of the white liquid into the palm of his sand-free hand and began to rub it gently over the smooth faultless skin. He enjoyed the hard, knobbiness of her spine from an aesthetic standpoint. It was perfect in its symmetry.

His eyes travelled forward to the long legs, and his thoughts returned to normal. He smoothed her shoulders and was about to transfer his attention to her thighs when she gently took the big tube from his left hand and began to finish the job by herself, which he thought a considerable pity.

She had had a strong urge, only just controlled, to let his hands feel her legs. She was sure, in the sensible part of her mind, that this was not the right attitude to have on a first acquaintance. Thinking over the problem in the warm heat of the sun, she quite rightly put the blame for the problem at the feet of the island.

Dacks showed her how to fit the mask over her face and adjusted the straps so that the rubber was tight to her skin without any gaps. He took it from her again and fitted the tube of the snorkel with its ping-pong ballcock at the top into the hole above the right eye so that the air would go into the mask leaving her nose and mouth free to breathe independently. His own mask had a cork in this place. The snorkel's mouth-grip fitted between his teeth, with the mask only covering his eyes and nose. It had taken him days of practice to breathe correctly through his adaptation, but it was more efficient when using the gun as otherwise the fast dive after a fish was inclined to jam the ping-pong ball and flood the mask.

He fitted the flippers on to her feet and adjusted the length so there was no movement. He put on his own black flippers and stood up in them with practised ease. He helped her to her feet with his left hand while still holding the masks and the loose snorkel in the other. He waved to the two sunbathers, put the snorkel and masks into his left hand and lobbed the 'Sea and Ski' to within a foot of Herman Small's suddenly very alarmed face. Then Dacks picked up the heavy spear-gun, loaded it by hooking the disc attached to his wrist on to the spear and pulling back strongly against the compressed air, and showed his 'new' interest how to walk over loose sand in flippers in a way that would prevent her from breaking her long and very sensual neck.

They got to the wet edge of the sea and he dipped the masks into the warm water, swilled them round, spat expertly into each one in turn and rubbed the spit onto the inside of the glass, spat again and repeated the exercise on the other side so as to stop the masks misting. He swilled the masks again in sea water and peered at the distant horizon through the clear thick glass. Satisfied, he fitted her mask over her head, flicked his own into place and looked at the green eyes through the magnification of their respective layers of unbreakable Italian glass.

He turned her round and walked with her backwards into the sea so that the flippers flowed with the tide. As she fell backwards and her costume became wet all over he remembered that he had always wanted to take a 'bunny girl' for a swim – and that here they were at last – *viva les gals.*

He put a strong arm around her waist and lifted her high above the sandy bottom and then gently put her down again so that her flippers rested evenly and her equilibrium was restored. The green eyes smiled at him from behind the oval of the glass. He was pleased to see that her mask was free of water slapping around her most enticing small and delicate mouth.

They successfully waded out into deeper water by going backwards. Dacks slowly leaned back into the water and let his feet float and body turn over. He put his masked face down into the water, spat out an inch of water from his snorkel and then breathed easily. He glanced around him at the clear world of the marine life, let his feet come down on to the deeper bottom and stood up. The water streamed off his hair and tanned face as he looked round for the 'bunny', Anna-Marie. The water was up to her waist but she was still slowly walking backwards. He let his feet float up off the sand and then moved them strongly against the pressure of the flippers.

He glided towards the exposed back with the smell of sea water and snorkel firmly in his nostrils. The thoughts of other pleasures were also firmly in his calculating mind. He smiled to himself and chuckled deep into his mask but not even the small fish swimming along down below had heard him. Part of the glass oval of his mask was sufficiently above the water to enable him to watch above and below the surface, and to guide himself and the gun, now light at his side as it was buoyed up by the sea water, towards his vantage point. At the last moment he flipped sideways and let his free left arm circle her slim waist so that it felt the lacework of her costume that had filled out with water and separated from the smooth silk of her skin underneath. His pleasure was acutely sensual. His arm gripped her as he swam away. She left the seabed and followed him out to sea, relaxing in the warm balm of the Indian Ocean. She had no alternative.

He swam on his back and was able to see the pressure of water building up in the soft cups of her bra and pushing them away from the two small but delightful shapes inside. He agreed with himself that the costume was not made for spear fishing but concluded that with only the two of them drawing further and further from the beach propriety was saved.

"Work your flippers, Anna-Marie... That's it. Now I'll let you float by yourself. When you feel buoyant enough, turn on to your stomach, and look down into the sea."

Slowly she floated away and then turned over and her face and mask looked down into the ocean. The bent end of her snorkel with its little cage gently furrowed the surface above her almost submerged hair.

He glided away to swim beside her and watched the same patch of the moving sea. A two-foot clam, fixed to its coral bed, was waiting for food with its jaws open and its muscle pulsing with life between jagged, beautiful pearl-white fangs. Three black zebra fish, flat, small and delicately finned, swam past the pulsing jaws and into the swaying tentacles of a mauve sea-anemone. The mauve tentacles let the fish swim in and out of its jellied myriad of fingers with pleasure and affection. It looked like a trap. Blue mounds of new, growing coral and fingers of little red tree coral grew next to each other and black, slug-like squid lay comfortably in between, rolling from side to side gently in the slow swell of the warm and sun-filled sea.

He floated his free left hand out to hers and guided her along on top of a deep channel so that her feet wouldn't touch the soft-looking beauty of the viciously sharp coral. The coral grew more and more thickly as they swam away from the sand that had built up over the years on the coral base close to the island.

A boxfish, flat on four sides and with a snout for a face, watched them with large, evil eyes as they glided by overhead, their long shadows playing on the coral and fish below. The boxfish would have been very poisonous to eat.

Dacks guided her round so that together they swam parallel with the island, a hundred yards off shore. The bed of the sea was ten feet below them but the coral grew up to six feet in places. Around these underwater hills were the fish. Yellow rainbow fish that were almost transparent and which lost their colour immediately when out of the water; parrot fish with big sucking lips; and a bright yellow fish with black spots even up on its gills, the leopard fish. The current drifted them past the clean, uncluttered grace of the ocean and Dacks had no wish to use his gun for anything but protection. There was no effort in the lazy flap, flap of their feet. Their bodies bent only gently at the knees. They breathed easily through the snorkels.

The channel deepened. On one side a coral cliff rose almost to the surface. The coral bulged out at the top near to the surface, but down below the sea had eaten into the layers of rock-coral and had left caves and ledges, some too dark to see into.

The inner reef took them out to sea. The fish grew larger and the bream more numerous. Dacks eased his thumb on to the safety catch of his gun and pushed forward as a shadow drifted across on his right. He turned his head and mask slowly so as not to bubble the water and obscure his vision, and looked straight into the half-open jaws of a four-foot grey shark that had no right to be inside the coral reef. The shark shut its jaws. He flicked off the safety catch, let go of the girl's hand and turned the whole of his body to face the small shark and discourage any ploy. He checked that the spear was in its right position and felt the heavy cord that fed on to his reel and gave him a range of thirty underwater feet. Motionless, they watched each other.

Anna-Marie turned to see why she had lost his hand and froze as the cold shark eyes took in her limbs and flesh. Her instinct was to swim away, but the fear of the unknown behind her was stronger than that in front. She put all her trust in the big body in the navy blue bathing trunks and the strange gun it held. As she waited while she felt the tide and current float her in towards the coral cliff with its jagged sides and beautiful colours and dark sombre underside.

The shark drifted with them. Dacks waited for the one and only shot he was allowed in underwater fishing while he calculated how much damage the razor-sharp teeth of the baby grey shark could do with one bite and a tear, and decided that it was better for them both if he didn't allow the sleek, oily, fin-topped length of hunger to try its luck. He must kill first.

He became more conscious of the current drifting him towards the dark rocks and knew that his room for manoeuvre was getting smaller by the second.

The shark moved in closer, still facing him, eyes cold and mouth shut. A difficult shot. Dacks held his finger on the trigger and waited, looking down on the fish four feet below the surface. He sensed the rock cliff behind him and considered the idea of a quick dive to below the shark's belly, a twist up and a gut shot, then remembered the girl and the consequences for her if he didn't succeed. So instead he was forced to wait for the shark to make its mistake. The shark knew better and stopped.

The drift continued. With the rock face feeling close behind him now, Dacks calculated the girl to be only a few feet from coral that would tear her flesh like flakes of wet paper. His decision made, he took a deep breath and dived straight at the shark. The shark flipped its tail and moved up to meet him. He brought down the gun and gauged the right trajectory against the shark's movement and the current's pull. He swam faster and kicked his feet viciously to frighten the shark. The twenty yards shortened to five. The jaws of the fish flashed open and the shark showed its belly as it struck. The spear leapt out of its socket. The barb furrowed a brief, vicious moment and smacked into the soft white underbelly.

The shark rolled and rolled at the end of the heavy cord line attached to the gun. Blood stained the white bib under the jaws. Another steel spear shot past two inches away from Dacks's nose at forty miles an hour, well away from the dying shark, and jerked itself up at the end of its line. Dacks slowly turned his head and followed the cord back along its trajectory. He came face to masked face with Harold Ackit. His 'guest' was crouching against a ledge of the cliff some ten feet below the water with a two-cylinder aqualung strapped to his back and a spent spear-gun in his hands.

Dacks powered himself to the surface with the definite thought in his mind that it was a good thing that a spear gun had only one shot. The dead shark rose with him on the end of his line. The spear had penetrated its lungs and the intrusion of its own blood had choked it to the final conclusion of a suffocating death. Dacks broke the surface and expertly spat out the full nine inches of water from his snorkel in one clean go and breathed a warm sweet draught of air into his burning lungs. Harold Ackit broke surface some ten yards away. From the beach, the three humans looked like humps on the smooth sea's surface. Harold Ackit pushed the tube that led from his oxygen cylinder out of his mouth.

"I didn't think you'd got him, Mark."

"You nearly got me."

"Sorry, but I had to take the chance. Borrowed the damn gun from Diogo and haven't had enough practice. Nasty things, sharks."

'You can say that again,' thought Dacks, taking the very cold hand of the very frightened Anna-Marie as he turned to begin the swim on down the channel towards a strong, very alcoholic drink. The southern tip of the island was the private domain of Diogo de Almeida and his very close or intimate friends. Dacks looked back once at a now indistinguishable Harold Ackit. Dacks had made up his own mind.

"Thanks for trying, Harold. Stick around there and you'll get plenty of practice with the bream."

He put the snorkel back into his mouth and immersed his face and mask in the water. He looked around for any of their dead companion's relatives. The only fish in sight were very colourful and very small. The thought of the blood-run behind him from the towed shark was not encouraging and with his only spear in the shark's belly, he hoped very sincerely for no more takers until they'd reached the steps that led up to the terrace of Diogo de Almeida's private house. It was the one building on which no money at all had been spared, and the others were luxuriously built. When Diogo de Almeida had found he was going to be cut off from the world he'd declared that he would only be cut off in comfort, and that being said, the materials had begun to arrive, and continued to do so for five years. Dacks had flown down especially for the house-warming party and spent the following day in bed as a result.

Anna-Marie took comfort from the strong hand gripping her very much smaller one and tried to forget the shark behind them and the man in his black rubber suit, who had taken careful aim at Mark Dacks and fired when he had seen that the shark was far more dead than alive. She wondered what else there was about the man beside her that made an apparent friend wish to kill him. She squeezed his hand and felt protected. She had come to Santa Salina to find excitement, and when she'd heard that Mark Dacks was on the island she had known there would be some interesting evenings if she could only meet him. But she hadn't been looking for her excitement in quite the way she had just experienced.

DACKS HELPED her grip the concrete and together they held themselves steady against the small jetty by floating on their stomachs and working their flippers behind them.

Dacks turned onto his back, drew in his knees and black flippers, and seated himself comfortably on a step that was some twelve inches below the water level. Holding the spear gun in one hand, he removed his flippers, put them on a dry step at shoulder height behind him, stood up and walked backwards up the flight of steps. The bottom of the flight of steps was concrete, but quickly changed to marble above the high-water mark. The smooth coolness of the highly-polished marble was welcome under his feet.

He stopped for a moment and looked out to sea. He had the same view as the multi-coloured house on its rise of coral rock behind him. Dacks wound the shark in and floated it onto a submerged step, walked down to his kill, gripped it by the jaws and pulled it up to the first step out of the water, clipped back the barb of his spear, which had pierced right through the fish, and pulled out the unimpeded steel shaft. He wound the cord on to the big reel and clipped the spear into place without loading the gun, then put down the four-foot contraption next to his mask, snorkel and flippers.

He dived back into the sea, swam round and in to the gently moving flippers at the end of a gently moving body, and helped Anna-Marie to remove her flippers. He managed to prevent himself from exploring further up her leg by concentrating hard on the rubber flippers. Then he climbed out of the water, put his right hand down to hers and lifted her up the steps past the dead shark and the spear-fishing equipment. Her black hair had fallen down below her shoulders and streamed water. The tension fell away as he put an arm around the slim black-laced waist and led her up to the grotesque statues that dominated the head of the steps as they looked out to sea. Anna-Marie instinctively drew away from the eight-foot cricket with two-foot antennae, pushing Dacks towards the eight-foot ant with eyes the size of cricket balls in black alabaster that stood stolidly on the other side. Dacks chuckled.

"Sorry, these two are the more gruesome side of Signor de Almeida's hobby. The experts say they are good for an amateur. If the intention was to create fear then he certainly succeeded. His talent extends to gentler sculpture too, as you can see over there along his Roman wall. He carved that Venus on the other side of the patio out of a single piece of marble. And even though her rear is a little out of proportion and I'm sure she has a squint, the rest is passable, especially if you know what his leanings are in relation to the female form. All this chipping away costs him a fortune but it gives him something to hammer at. I think sculpting is a mixture of aesthetic taste and the desire to be hurt and to hurt. If you hammer that marble the wrong way all the vibrations run straight back up the chisel and all but tear off your arm. If you hit the right way, bits of marble fly all over the place."

"Is that him making the noise on the other side of the house?"

"It seems as though we have caught him in one of his moments of creation. If we go across and take that path between the Roman pillars, and stand behind that distant large Grecian urn you can just see at the far end, we can observe without being observed. Then we'll come back and investigate his refrigerator and the contents of his cocktail cabinet."

Dacks led the way past the cupid fountain plummeting water back into a white marble bowl at the young archer's feet that was held there at arm's length by a young firm-bosomed nymph. The contrast between this and the eight-foot monsters guarding the route to the sea was startling. There were no flowers on the terrace, nor anything else growing at all. The low walls, which could be easily looked over to see down to the sea, were a softer white granite and had been carved more roughly to achieve the required contrast with the numerous statues sitting, standing and fighting around the perimeter of the marble expanse of the Greco-Roman patio.

Dacks was pleased to see the long swing-couch, covered on three sides by a canvas decorated in the style of a Florentine fresco. He knew also that the 'love-swing' could be asked, with the firm press of a button, to close up in the front. It stood on feet splayed sympathetically to the rest of the ornamentation, with its long white mattress and rounded white cushions.

Dacks looked back at Anna-Marie and felt a small electric surge of expectancy run its way up from the depths of his stomach. The small hand in his felt very much softer and the green eyes just a shade more exciting. He concluded that the long black hair needed a definite stroke, as did the rest of her body.

Anna-Marie touched a fluted column with its flat round top some four feet above her head, and found it to be solid and carved. She had seen imitations before but none that hadn't been poured instead of being carved, like this one, from a single block of granite. Her other hand was conscious of the feeling she was generating in the tall, darkly tanned man next to her and the expectancy in herself was as great, though she didn't recognise the feeling as surely as he did. She looked sideways at him, caught his eye and softly smiled. She was rewarded by his right eyebrow rising and falling a fraction of an inch. He squeezed her hand and she returned the pressure as they slunk up behind the vast Grecian urn with the sound of hammering growing considerably stronger in their ears.

By leaning out to sea and looking round the fluted belly of the urn they were rewarded with the sight of an inordinately happy Diogo de Almeida, large hammer in one hand, nine-inch pointed chisel in the other, a long smock over his shoulders and down to his ankles with gaps for his well-tanned mahogany arms, chipping and hammering away at a chunk of marble twice his size. His endeavours were sending the chips and fine dust over everything, but in particular over himself. A white layer had covered his face and black curly hair and changed him completely to resemble an ancient doyen of the ancient arts. The marble block still had no recognisable form but this was no deterrent to the flying chips. On the sea wall to Diogo de Almeida's right, in easy line with his eyes and some ten feet away, was a two-foot clay model of a young girl in a bikini that looked familiar to Dacks. He studied it more carefully; it was the expression and the stance that made it most recognisable to him, rather than its likeness to the flesh.

Dacks turned his attention back to Diogo's ongoing efforts and tried to imagine a bikini-clad Korina Prague standing ten feet tall in white marble. The idea of so much Korina Prague was certainly satisfying but it didn't prevent him from leading Anna-Marie away from the maestro's studio, along the same path between Roman pillars on to the same soft smoothness of marble patio. He felt a twinge of conscience but forcibly overcame his weakness.

He led her across the main patio and into the lounge with its large mouth of open sliding doors that gulped in the cooler air from the sea. By instinct he bent down and released the flap of the cocktail cabinet, which contained the refrigerator. The hour was almost twelve and drinking perfectly permissible.

He selected a bottle of soda water and a long frosted glass that contained crushed mint and transferred them both to the open flap of the cocktail cabinet in front of the assorted array of drinks bottles, at least two of which had only been sampled as part of a bet. Dacks turned his eyes away from a Dutch plum liqueur which he remembered too well and selected a full bottle of Booths gin from which he expertly removed the foil and unclipped the cap.

He put the glass cocktail shaker with its silver-cone top in between the mint and the gin and placed two long glasses next to the soda water. Without using a measure, he gurgled the slightly yellow liquid into the shaker until the gin bottle had lost a sixth of its very expensive imported content. He clipped the top into place and put the bottle back with the others out of harm's way.

Using a bobble-ended glass swizzle stick, he helped the mint out of the frosted glass and into the gin, then watched the crushed leaves sink below the alcoholic surface. Then, using the bottle opener, he clipped off the cap of the soda bottle, put his thumb over the open top, lifted it out to arm's length, and shook it vigorously. He then held the bottle upside down over the open shaker and eased his thumb off the top. The pressurised soda water shot at the gin for five hissing seconds. Satisfied, Dacks put the empty bottle down, selected five large ice cubes from the refrigerator, plopped them in as well, fitted the silver top with its silver cap onto the shaker, extended a bent arm with the shaker in front of him and commenced to flick his wrist. The slosh of ice, soda and gin was very interesting if a little menacing to Anna-Marie, who stood watching him in her now dry bathing costume.

He put the bottoms of the two stemmed glasses together carefully in his right hand, picked up the shaker in the same grip and put his free arm around Anna-Marie's well-made waist. With expert guidance, he led her out of the lounge towards the 'love-swing' which had two other names, one given it by Diogo de Almeida, the other, a fraction less vulgar, by Dacks.

The white linen covers were without blemish or crease and stretched exactly over the square cushions and wide buoyant mattress. The sun shone from behind, but the Florentine frescoed cover was heavy enough to keep out the brunt of the heat while, at the same time, permitting the sea breeze to run in underneath the two-foot gap between canvas and marble to cool any prostrate occupants of the swing-couch.

He and Anna-Marie sat next to each other, with Dacks nearest the ledge that was fixed to the stand, specially made to take two glasses and the cocktail shaker. With a final flip of ice against metal and glass, he removed the small cylindrical cap on the metal cone and poured the mint julep through the strainer into the long glasses, which immediately frosted with the contact of ice-cold liquid and warm air. He gave her a glass. They drank quietly and with appreciation. The cool liquid in his own glass drained down his throat with one pour and he was pleased to see hers do almost the same. He refilled the glasses and they started again. Then he stretched back and brought his feet over and behind her. His big left toe easily found the button, and immediately the front canvas dropped down and sealed them from the outside as Anna-Marie leaned back across his chest and let him take her half-empty, now unnecessary glass from her. He placed it next to his own on the ground in the pre-arranged way to show anyone who was likely to come on to the patio that the Florentine frescoed swing was occupied. Finally, he permitted both his hands a long search of her body, then folded her costume down below her navel as a prelude for more pleasures to come.

12

AN ISLAND INDABA

The *Cara Mia* moved across the night sea towards Bagota island at a steady fifteen knots. There was a good moon. The sky was cloudless and the black dome of the heavens was studded with celestial diamonds, some small, some large.

Gabe Saunders was at the wheel while Yasani slept in the fighting chair, his legs splayed out in the direction of the bait box with his head lolling gently from the slight roll of the *Cara Mia* at less than half speed. There were no lights on the boat and the low speed enabled the engines to run with the smallest amount of noise.

Inside the cabin, Dacks was stretched out on one side of the wall-seat and Diogo de Almeida, free of marble dust, was on the other. They were wearing shorts with a small gun in the right-hand pocket of one pair and a larger gun in the right-hand pocket of the other, and their feet stuck up. The large feet of Diogo de Almeida's were bathed in moonlight. The heat was oppressive but they were both too idle to go up on deck to cool off. Both of them were recovering from the exhaustion of their respective pleasures.

There was a small smile in the left-hand corner of Dacks's mouth. Without moving his head, he turned his wrist and read the illuminated dials of his watch and estimated the boat, and the sack of currency transferred from Diogo de Almeida's safe to the locker underneath his head, to be five minutes away from the island with its inland lakes and crocodiles and hippos that had interbred in a small community ever since the island broke itself away from the mainland mass some twenty thousand years before. His mind reverted to Harold Ackit and the fact that Yasani had found nothing unusual in his baggage, not even the transmitter. He was certain that the man had tried to kill him and not the shark. He was nearly sure in his mind that Harold Ackit had written him the letter at the Casino Hotel and had even called in his friend from the police, knowing by then that the emeralds would be in his room. But even in all of this he found it difficult to reconcile the old and trusted firm of London bankers, Messrs Cornell and Ackit, with the practices he knew were encouraged by the group who operated the illicit diamond trade in Central and South Africa. He cast his mind back to Harold Ackit's partner and remembered nothing that didn't fit the image of a City banker. The matter was a puzzle that had given him nothing definite to point his finger at and therefore nothing definite against which to take precautions.

He relaxed his body more completely and once again considered the problem of getting machinery to Sofala in Mozambique with only himself and a few members of the tribe in full possession of the facts. He had also become concerned with the problem of the tribe spending the large amount of money that was reposing so innocently just below his head. If spent out of hand, the authorities would surely recognise it as not coming from agriculture. His thoughts went further over the problem and led him to the formation of a new company that would purchase goods on behalf of the tribe and then forward them to the required final destination. In this way, no one besides himself and the buyer in the tribe would know where the goods were going. His records would show an assortment of buyers' names that would mean nothing collectively on paper. The suppliers in Salisbury and elsewhere would only have invoices made out to the Farmers Buying Company Limited, and there were many such buying companies in Salisbury. He could even do a little outside buying as a blind. Then he realised that he could also use this new company for the machinery and make it appear to the suppliers as though the items were going all over the country. He knew that all these points had to be thought of to prevent someone becoming suspicious and leading them to the main operation.

He chuckled to himself and wondered just how much went on in such a material world that appeared so honest on the surface but was anything but underneath.

He felt the cartridge cylinder of his .22 target pistol inside his right-hand pocket and wondered whether he should go in for soft-nose bullets. No, he finally decided. Too messy. He glanced at his watch and heaved his feet over the side of the seat. The dead weight pulled his head up. He sat up and rubbed the back of his head, while Diogo de Almeida began to breathe a little more heavily.

Dacks made his way to the refrigerator at the juncture of the seat surrounds, quietly opened the door, pulled out a cold water bottle and, with difficulty, made his way around to the other side of the central table and poured half the contents of the water bottle over the dark face of Diogo de Almeida. The breathing remained constant but the mouth came open, just visible in the light of the moon, and the water that hit this gap merely sank, its loss marked by the jagged movement of the sculptor's hard-working Adams apple.

Dacks swigged a little of the water himself, shrugged his shoulders and moved to the three steps out of the cabin, walked up them and emptied the last of the ice-cold water over Yasani, waking him. Across the water, he could see the dark smudge of the island. It was totally dark and there were no fires to be seen. Behind him, Gabe Saunders cut the engine to a crawling speed and the bows of the *Cara Mia* sank down into the water and the craft wallowed its way in the slight swell towards the long hump of the island.

The island split into separate hills and inlets as they drew closer. In one cove a small pinpoint of chilling light became visible. The

Cara Mia changed direction slightly. The light grew stronger and the dark night-shrouded island of Bagota drew them into the land.

Gabe Saunders judged his landmarks carefully, the swollen hump on the one side and the single, giant rock, separate from the island on the other. He changed directions twice to avoid the sandbars and finally took them into the bay and cut his engines. The lap of water on the metal hull was soft. The small fire burning on the beach was sharply visible as its flames rose and fell. The people standing back from the shore merged with the cliff and could only be seen with difficulty or when they moved. The moon was behind the cliff and its shadow formed high over their heads. Dacks knew that they would all move inland for the Indaba, away from the eyes of boats and unwanted people. These people had come to welcome him.

The iron anchor went over the side and dropped the six feet through the water into the sand. The leeway of the *Cara Mia* was brought up gently at the end of the chain.

Diogo de Almeida appeared in the cabin doorway with the sacks of money gripped one in each hand. Dacks followed him forward and together they lowered the dinghy into the sea and towed it to the stern. All four of them got in, Dacks taking one sack and Diogo de Almeida keeping hold of the other.

Yasani pulled the starter rope and the two-stroke Seagull engine phut-phutted into life, and immediately the dinghy moved away from the black craft that was left gently tugging at its anchor chain.

Fifty yards later, they hit bottom. Gabe Saunders jumped out and held the boat steady and then swung it sideways to the shore while the others got out.

Dacks walked up the beach over the soft white moon-bathed sand and raised his right arm with the flat of his hand open and towards the people in shadow behind the fire. He exchanged words in Ndebele with Joseph's father and murmurs of approval spread in both directions from behind the fire and the people converged on him as he went from one to the other, slapping hands, grasping hands firmly and then immediately letting go. Diogo de Almeida,

Gabe Saunders and Yasani followed behind him in the same procedure.

Dacks followed Joseph's father away from the sea and they began to climb up a small path between two junctures of cliff with the others behind them in a crocodile line. There was no sound as they moved barefoot. Dacks turned and looked back at the beach but the fire had been put out. The *Cara Mia* was a black uniform patch on the sea, silvered by the moon and warmed by the soft tropical air that had taken its heat from the mainland of Africa not fifteen miles to the west.

As they walked higher, the breeze became cooler and reminded Dacks that he purposely hadn't eaten for twelve hours. He began to look forward to the celebrations ahead. The canvas sack of money in his right hand had become heavy, despite its paper content. He decided to get the business side over with quickly so that they could all get on with the eating and drinking.

Inland, the end of Bagota to which they were walking was shaped like a saucer. With the breeze from behind them they saw the fires first as they topped the path. They could see the spitted game, and a little further on down, they smelt the cooking kudu, wild pig and buffalo. There were lines of stone jars away from the fires that contained maize beer. Hanging from the trees were open-pored canvas bags that dripped water and contained large bottles of Laurentina beer keeping cool for the guests and for the younger men with modern tastes.

Dacks permitted his tongue to run over his lips as the smell of the spit-cooked game reached his nostrils for the fourth time. A certain pleasure also rose at the glint of a bottle-neck sticking out, waiting for him, from its cooling bag.

The drums beat as they moved towards a tarpaulin that had been stretched out between two fires. The surface glinted in small mounds and brought Dacks to an amazed halt some ten yards short of the display. The twelve-foot-square sheet was covered in mounds of precious stones and the fire played its light among the twinkling crystals and made him quickly conclude that the weight hanging from his right hand, even combined with that carried by Diogo, was by no means enough. He further concluded that Joseph's father, the *ngaka*, was indeed a wizard. He took up his position cross-legged on one side of the diamonds and opposite another friend, Mnzedi, who was sitting in the same way. It was Mnzedi who had first come to Dacks with the problem of selling the tribe's diamonds, but at the time neither had suspected the tribe would find so much wealth. Dacks waited for him to speak.

"I think we can say that this year we have collected a lot of diamonds and though this light is not good, I can assure you they are all of the good colours."

"I'll take your word for it as usual. I don't know so much about this side myself but as you know, if I make too much money when I sell them again, you get most of it back. In this business it is necessary to trust or otherwise everything is no good. I have brought ten thousand pounds with me. Some of the money is in Escudos, some in Nyasaland pounds, some in Congolese Francs, some in Zambian pounds, but most is in the pounds of our country, Mnzedi. I can see from the stones in front of me that this is not enough. It has been told to me that you want machinery to make a deep mine and that you have friends from the South African mines to work these machines. I will supply these free up to an amount that will be set by the experts in England when they have given me a true value for these stones. We are going to have a rich tribe if the machinery digs up more like this. From now it will be better for you to ask me to buy for you the goods that are needed or else we will have many people asking many questions."

"That will be done. It is a good system."

"I will leave here the money. You will know how to split this among the kraals."

They switched from English to Ndebele and discussed the less private matters of food and crops and rain. The stones were put into the money-sacks and the money was left on the tarpaulin. Then long curved hunting knives were passed to each person; the stone jars were opened; the beer bottles taken from the cooling canvasses;

the drums beat; the reed pipes played the same four notes; again and again; the chanting and dancing began and slices were cut from the cooking carcasses and eaten straight away.

TWO HOURS LATER, there was a considerable amount of potential drunkenness and some forty-eight bellies were full of food. The fires had been heaped regularly with new wood. Everyone, including Dacks and his three companions, had played the drums, blown the pipes and plucked the locally-made guitars. Dacks was on his fourth litre-sized bottle of Laurentina lager and Diogo de Almeida was on his sixth. Delicately, Dacks removed a cut from the right shoulder of the upside-down, feet-jutting-upwards, very well roasted kudu, fed it into his mouth and chewed it with the required amount of appreciation. He was glad that he had only worn shorts and shirt, as the saucer arrangement of the island kept in the heat and kept out the breeze.

The rattle of small arms explosions from the surrounding hills sent his right hand into his pocket and found him the only one standing at the party. The others had sensibly thrown themselves to the ground. He let the gun in his hand traverse the dark lip of the hills. The silence and darkness immediately making him feel his inadequacies. He realised they were surrounded and picked out in perfect silhouette by the well-stacked fires around and behind them. He cursed himself for not having left a guard on the *Cara Mia* and wished that the almost seven pints of beer inside him were back in their bottles with the caps unlevered. He waited, and the night went on around him and the fires burned just as brightly as before. The sack of diamonds and the pile of bank notes seemed particularly naked and beyond his control.

He noticed Yasani begin to glide away on his stomach but heard the shot and saw the body jerk before he could shout for him to stop. They were easy targets and the night was all around them. He didn't have to go over and stand beside one of his best men to find out whether he was dead. He looked away and up at the hills and then realised they were not surrounded by the police. He looked back to Yasani's body, lying with its face in the dry earth, its legs twisted in sudden pain and death, and vowed to take many eyes for the two dead eyes and many teeth for Yasani's. There was a hatred in him for the first time. The game was no longer a game, the pleasure was no longer with him, the reward for all of them had been lost in that one explosion that had given death which had no means of being purchased in reverse. He had a deadly revenge in his gut and the power of many men for destruction. He switched his thoughts into Ndebele and addressed the people around him.

"Everyone stay as you are. Our friend, Yasani, is dead. They can see us too easily and they are not the police. There is too much wealth in our midst. Among ourselves there was no need for it to be guarded, but someone outside of us has had word of this money and has come to steal it from us. What they steal now we can take back later. If we fight now they will kill many of us and still have the stones and the money. It is my wish that everyone must lie still. The spirit of Yasani has left us and we all think of him this moment and know that he will remain in the night as a spirit of good, but that the man who killed him will remain as nothing but dead bones and dead flesh when I have killed him later. Rest all assured that our friend will be avenged in this life as well as in the life of the spirits."

He pointed his gun high above his head at the stars and pulled the trigger six times and walked towards the previous gunfire in the wake of the echoes from his own .22. He reverted in his mind to English.

"This is Mark Dacks. I suspect that if it is someone you want then that someone is me. The gems and the money you can see. If you kill all these people you will have many of their relatives to avoid for the rest of your lives and Africa is a place that holds no secrets, as you have proved tonight. It is better for you to take the stones and leave only one man's blood on your hands."

He kept walking towards the hills that were bathed in moonlight and yet showed nothing, and waited for the shot, prepared to throw himself sideways on to the ground.

A bitter chuckle echoed from some hundred yards out in front of him.

"I can see this is going to be a good night for me. First I take your two women and now I have you, Mark Dacks. A very good night. Put your hands slowly on your head and keep coming, Mr Dacks. It is you we want, Mr Dacks. A paltry ten thousand pounds is nothing to us and the gems are no good to your friends without you, and they won't have you any longer. Oh... And don't think too hard. I have an excruciating desire to cut some of the beautiful skin from Miss Prague's face and it would also satisfy me to do even better things to your little pleasure from Vienna. They were so charming about coming with us but that is often how life goes. It often looks so good... And then comes the crunch. Keep walking. We will take care of Signor de Almeida and Mr Saunders some other time unless they leave Africa very quickly and fail to return. Your system is over, Mr Dacks... Keep walking. How does it feel, walking to your death? The sharks will be pleased, and I'm sure that before being fed to them you'll grant me the pleasure of carving up your pretty little girls and making them do my will. While you watch, of course."

Dacks suddenly thought of his liaison with Anna-Marie being explained to Korina and did not look forward to the consequences. The problem, he concluded, was one he'd need all his guile to overcome. Jealous women he found difficult to placate and especially Korina Prague, as he'd learnt to his cost on four previous occasions. Men will be men, he told himself, but the ring of his voice in his mind was hollow and didn't uncoil the problem in his stomach. He turned his mind back to the second problem and decided that he would be able to do nothing until he could see his adversaries. Fighting in the dark with a light at his back was a form of suicide and Dacks intended to kill and not be killed.

The man in front of him breathed heavily and with asthmatic difficulty as Dacks came to a halt at the end of the wheezer's rifle. There was no plan in Dacks's mind except waiting for an opportunity that he fully realised, with a large number of well-loaded rifles pointing at various parts of his anatomy, was not to be found in the present.

"You have the most interesting method of breathing. With a little assistance I would say it could be encouraged to stop altogether."

"Shut up."

"Very rude... But then to be expected."

Dacks accepted the pain in his ribs as the butt of a rifle thudded into his chest with a twitched chuckle, which only encouraged a second blow on his other side.

"My sadistic tendencies are not limited to women," Ackit informed him. "I also enjoy inflicting pain on the men who are liked by the women. You can call it a sop to my jealousy. You can, in fact, call it whatever you like, but I enjoy it so very much just the same. It is what I like about power. I like confronting people with it; with this little thought in your mind, I would like to take you to your friends who are sitting so apprehensively on my boat at the moment. They had a certain kind of fear in their eyes which told me I would not be disappointed. I like the real me to come out and tomorrow it will. All of it. I will play with you all for my pleasure. There must always be pleasure out of hard work and you have given us plenty of this in the last few years. They sent me out to learn who you were, and now that I've found out all about you and your dear little girls I want my reward. I have a very strong perversion, you see, that needs to be satisfied."

With another asthmatic intake of breath, Ackit stood up and signalled the butt smasher away from Dacks. They walked away from the fires some hundred yards behind them and the shadows of night fell into their pattern of movement. There was only one man unconscious of their going and Dacks had no intention of his being forgotten. He had his peculiar perversions, too, when it came to avenging cold-blooded murder.

13

FLYING KNIVES

Dacks was not given even a small chance by his antagonists when they took him down to the shore. He had been taken to the side of the island where Gabe Saunders had moored the *Cara Mia*. Dacks was relieved that his friends had been sensible and had not tried to attack his well-armed guard. However carefully it might have been planned, hunting knives and two revolvers taken onto the beach for the celebrations were no match for twenty rifles.

He wasn't, therefore, surprised to still find himself a captive as he walked across the last stretch of the beach. He got into the dinghy unaided and was taken out towards the large craft he could see a half mile out to sea. The thought crossed his mind that Ackit hadn't found the *Cara Mia*, which they had moored close to the shore. If looked at from out to sea, he hoped it would have merged with the island and appeared part of the land.

This was his hope as the small launch bumped the metal side of the big craft. It took him one glance to classify the ship as a converted motor-torpedo boat. He guessed its maximum speed at forty knots and remembered, again with the smallest particle of hope, Gabe Saunders's quiet confidence that with all his tuning he would be able to get forty-eight knots out of the *Cara Mia*.

Dacks, his mind for a moment in constructive thought, was roughly pulled up over the iron railings that surrounded the deck, then propelled towards the hatch.

Inside the corridor, having cracked both his elbows descending the vertical stairs after further unwanted propulsion from behind, he was pushed into a large spacious cabin. He was not surprised to see Harold Ackit already comfortable in a chair sipping a long drink from an expensive glass. Neither was he surprised to see the sprawled bodies of Korina Prague and Anna-Marie. They were draped in armchairs, their arms and legs thrown out in limp abandonment. They had both been left in their pants and bras, but nothing else. Dacks strained to get free to get at Ackit, but Ackit remained aloof and untouched. In final frustration Dacks vented his feelings by swearing at them all from the gutter of his vocabulary.

"Don't be so upset, Mark. They're not dead. They gave us a little fight and had their clothes torn off, but apart from that and the drugs, they're just as you left them. I haven't touched them yet. I wanted you to hear their screams when I did that. I thought your jealousy would add to my pleasure."

Harold Ackit lazily got up and affectionately stroked Korina Prague's disarrayed hair. He looked at her in soft expectancy and then let his hand drop to his side. He turned and faced Dacks and his expression was cruel and vicious. There was no resemblance between this man and the one Dacks had known before.

"You filthy bastard," Dacks shouted.

"Hit him, Norman. I don't like to be sworn at."

The knee in his groin was hard and accurate and the violent pain contorted his face before he could control it. He swiftly unbent himself and looked puzzled for Harold Ackit's benefit when the joining of his head and Norman's jaw made a violent crack.

Norman spat out half a tooth and kicked him in the groin again. At the same time, his partner twisted Dacks's arm up behind his back and prevented him from returning to a tooth-extraction position. Dacks was forced to remain with his head twelve inches above the cabin floor. The floor was dirty.

"Give the girls another injection to wake them up," Harold Ackit told Norman, "and then we will get on with our little bit of fun and be away well before the sun comes up. I wish to be back in my room next to the other guests when it is still dark. We have four hours to play with, and then the fish will be able to feed. I seem to remember from my days of fishing in the ponds behind the coal dumps in England when I was a child that fish like to feed at first light. I expect the larger fish out here will have similar habits, or maybe in tropical waters they are hungry all the time for blood. Purely academic of course, but sometimes it is nice to know."

Norman found a syringe in the cupboard and pushed the needle through the cork and sucked a clear liquid out of a small, glass bottle. He tested the syringe for bubbles by expertly pointing it at the light bulb and squirting just a little from the needle. It gave him visible satisfaction. He bent to Anna-Marie's limp right arm, which hung over the side of the chair. He touched it smoothly with the tips of his fingers. His other hand went to her left breast and felt it softly before he suddenly pulled his hand away, grabbed the arm and viciously dug in the needle. There was no reaction from the drugged girl but Dacks felt the needle as though it had gone into himself. They had let him up to see the 'doctor' at his dual purpose. The same ritual then befell Korina Prague.

Dacks's mind ran through all the possibilities of attack, but he was forced to discard them in turn. He felt a cold sweat break out on his face as he realised he would be forced to watch their orgy and be unable to do anything. He knew that if it hadn't been for himself, the two girls would not now be facing rape and slow murder.

He felt the boat shudder and knew the engines were giving power. He waited and then confirmed to himself that they were under way.

Anna-Marie came round first and a pleasant smile spread over her face as she took in the company. Dacks wondered what filthy drug it was that they had used on her. Then Korina did the same and he knew there was no help to be had from them.

"Which one would you like first?" asked Harold Ackit.

Norman pointed at Anna-Marie. He went over to her and took a hand gently and lifted the same arm that he had previously, viciously jabbed.

"Come and stand over by the board, my dear."

He led her across the cabin and stood her against an improvised dartboard. The cork backing ran from the ceiling to the floor. She appeared to have no power to stop him. He stroked both her bare hips in a joint, downward motion full of a deep certainty of future pleasure, then stood back from her. She swayed slightly and Dacks realised she was still more than half under the sedative and that it was only the power of the energiser that had enabled her to walk and now stand. Norman went back and opened a small cupboard on the wall opposite the girl. Dacks knew immediately that the knives revealed inside were for throwing, as he'd mastered the art himself some years before.

"Put them both there together," interjected Harold Ackit. "If you damage the wall it doesn't matter, two such lovely figures side by side will look so much better than one. And it will test your skill even more, my friend. It may even make up for your stupidity at the Victoria Falls. Now, that looks better. My little Korina as well. Now, my dear friend, you may carry on, but do it slowly. Do it slowly. I want to have that one just before she is quite dead."

The almost naked, perfect female bodies stood facing the length of the cabin side by side. Anna-Marie's legs were longer and her hips more pronounced than Korina's softer, smoother legs and hips. The two girls seemed to have no power to move and the smiles of contented pleasure remained on their beautiful faces as Norman took the first, twelve-inch knife from the rack. Dacks could do nothing about it.

The gap of six inches between the girls narrowed and widened as the energiser fought to gain control of their bodies. The sway of the boat made the movement more pronounced. Korina's navel dilated and swelled as she breathed. The flesh around it was thick and firm. Anna-Marie's legs were slightly apart and the hard, expectant eyes of the knife thrower were fixed firmly at the top-most cavity of light below her deep orange pants, which only just stretched over that very firm part of her body and only up to halfway from the top of her hips.

The knife came back and flew straight and viciously at the inside of her right thigh, which was only saved by the sway of her body in pace with the ship's movement. The two sharp edges of the knife pointed up and down and as she swayed over to the opposite side of her pendulum, her soft, white flesh just at that part kissed and pressed into the quivering steel and the phallic symbol was realised in its ugliest form.

Norman took a second knife from the rack and the sound of his harsh breathing was mingled with lust. Harold Ackit's eyes were riveted on the still quivering first blade and the eighth of an inch above.

Dacks could feel the lust oozing its way down towards the other end of the room from the guards by his side. He felt their grips on him slacken as the second symbol of their animal, greatest pleasure quivered the wood panelling to the left of Korina Prague's sun-tanned neck. They both shuddered with pleasure as the wanted flesh swayed and kissed the shining steel that was almost immediately joined by another some six inches away to its right. Korina's head was pinned and only her hips rolled with the slight swell and heave of the motorboat. The knife blades were flat to her skin. As she pulled to the limit of her sway, she gave the cutting, top edge of the left-hand weapon a purchase on her pinched skin. Blood oozed over the blade and Norman stopped his fourth throw to take in this new pleasure to the full. The eyes of both girls were glazed and there was no sign of pain in their expressions.

Dacks was conscious of a growing chance of freedom and began again to closely judge the distances around the room. The male eyes, other than his own, were focused hungrily on the various strategic parts of the women's bodies and his scrutiny went unnoticed.

The fourth knife hit the boarding beside Anna-Marie's left hip and nicked her flesh in its passage. A fifth blade hit the other side and cut a piece from her orange pants. The three knives were in line with each other. The pants had lost their firm pull and had flapped open at the bottom, half an inch away from the previously hidden flesh. Blood ran down her leg on the other side. The sway of her hips was stopped by the pinioning knives. A sixth knife sliced into the boarding just above the fifth, but failed to cut the last strands of the material. The orange silk just held on to its secret.

The blade that furrowed between Korina Prague's closed legs cut her deeply on the right side and brought a gasp of surprise from her lips and a glance of recognition as she looked down in surprise and hurt at the intruder quivering in the newly spilt blood between her legs. Dacks realised that the shock had shortened the life of the drug. The outside edges of his hands came up open and flying and dug the air out of the windpipes of both his guards on either side of him as another knife went between Anna-Marie's armpits on its way to cutting her bra strap. The garment came loose and released the burden in its left side as the hard toe of Dacks's right shoe kicked the thrower into violent pain at the juncture of his spinal cord and the backs of his legs. Dacks's third movement ripped open his own shirt, as he extracted the thin-bladed knife from its sheath and brought the tip of the point up to the surprised Adam's apple of Harold Ackit who simultaneously dropped his expensive glass on the floor.

"Tell your friends not to move or I'll push this knife through your neck."

Dacks smiled at the cold fury in Harold Ackit's eyes and the sign of amusement made his guest's Adam's apple work even more furiously. He smiled at the two guards who were waiting for orders. They were getting none. Norman lay face down on the floor with both his hands clasped behind him and clutching his backside. He was making noises.

"All right, clever guy. We'll just wait," said Harold Ackit. "I'm sitting down and you're not, and if I want to there's nothing preventing me having a sleep. No one knows where we are so in the good of time my friends will overpower you and then we will be able to finish our game. Oh, now look at that. Both your little girls are losing blood. When they faint, as they will, they'll fall on those cleverly protruding blades and slice themselves right up the middle. It should be a reasonably satisfying way of watching them die if the worst comes to the worst. Oh, and if you were thinking of moving me out of here and up on deck, don't forget your back will at some point be to someone and a bullet kills faster than a knife. Then again, how do you keep this knife at my throat and help your pretty little friends before they reach the stage of no longer needing any? No, Mr Dacks, I'm afraid it is no good. This is my ship and on it you are one against too many. A pity the girls are drugged or else they might have been able to help you in here, and again with the dinghy up top; but as it is, it was necessary for us to drug them so that they would help us create this delightful little spectacle that you now see at the other end of this cabin. Yes, by the time I take my pleasure, they will have recovered enough to know what is happening, but still be too weak to take any action other than letting you hear their screams. Oh, and don't think your friend will ever find this boat, as we have changed course three times since we left the island and the ocean is very wide."

"We shall see about that," answered Dacks and though his voice sounded confident, his inner mind knew that time was still definitely on Harold Ackit's side.

Dacks began to think and the small, intricate cogs in his mind worked smoothly. Harold Ackit had been right. The girls were growing weaker and they were both oozing too much blood. He studied his means of travel around the room, gripped Harold Ackit by his hair and jerked viciously, the knife still steady against the sadist's throat. Harold Ackit stood up and immediately found himself being frog-marched around the left-hand perimeter of the cabin with Dacks's back to the wall and himself acting as a shield.

They reached Korina Prague first.

"Take the knife out, Harold and don't tear any more of her skin. Can you feel my knife? It is very sharp and will cut the skin around your scrawny, white neck very easily. For every drop of blood that leaves Korina, I will cut three from you, so be quick."

The flick of Dacks's right hand cut a deep slit in the side of Harold Ackit's neck, a quarter of an inch long. An eighth of an inch further in would have nicked his windpipe and allowed his life to seep out along with his blood.

Harold Ackit felt the power of the knife at his own throat, and jerked out the knife that protruded from between Korina's legs in a spasmed reflex of fear.

"Now the others. Drop that one first."

Five knives clattered onto the cabin floor. Dacks turned his back towards the same wall that framed the girls and pushed Harold Ackit on towards Anna-Marie. Korina was safe and for the moment he had no more time to spare. The banker had no need for a second invitation to a little of his own bloodletting and quickly released the knives around Anna-Marie. Her knees gave way slowly and she folded gently onto the floor.

Korina, still on her feet, managed a weak smile before she spoke in a toneless voice.

"I can think now, Mark, but I'll have to sit down. I'm weak and fuzzy and look at all this blood down me."

Korina walked away from the wall in a curve that eventually brought her up to Harold Ackit's chair. She sat down with a thump and her head slumped forward and her eyes stared down at her blood-stained thighs. There was no movement in her body after that.

Dacks began to calculate how far the motorboat had gone from the *Cara Mia*. Unless the *Cara Mia* had started by luck in the right direction, they would be well out of the twenty-mile radius of the *Cara Mia*'s radar that Harold Ackit had been careless enough not to recognise.

"Korina!" he snapped. "Grab the last of your strength, tear up your dress that's on the floor, bandage yourself and then bandage Anna-Marie. You've both lost enough blood. You must stop the bleeding."

Korina Prague did the job with many words of encouragement from Dacks. She sank back into the chair, still watched by the five men in the cabin. Dacks caught at the fading strength in her green eyes and smiled his own power into them and in so doing he drew out the last of her reserves. Dacks's will had fought the drug and won.

"Make yourselves comfortable, everyone," said Dacks, looking round the room. "We may have a long wait. The *Cara Mia* will find us and, for the moment, time is on our hands, Harold, and so I intend to let time take its course."

14

REVENGE

Harold Ackit and Mark Dacks looked up at the cabin roof simultaneously. There was no mistaking the sound. The high-pitched scream of the *Cara Mia* at full power became rapidly louder and then the pitch changed and they both knew that the motorboat had been recognised. Gabe Saunders knew all the boats in the Mozambique Channel and must have recognised the hired launch from Beira for what it was.

Inside the closed cabin they listened to the black launch as it circled them. Anna-Marie was sitting up. Norman was now lying on his back. The thin blade was firmly and comfortably within half an inch of Harold Ackit's jagged, scraggy Adam's apple. Dacks's brain was working quickly and in many directions.

"Who are you?" came to them muffled from the *Cara Mia*'s loudhailer.

Harold Ackit cursed his upstairs crew's stupidity for not replying. If he had been up top, he told himself angrily, he could have bluffed them in minutes and had them innocently streaming away from their quarry.

Dacks looked at Korina hopefully but discarded the idea of her taking up his throat-cutting position over Harold Ackit. She was still too weak and too drugged. Anna-Marie was holding her own, but nothing more. On glancing back at Norman, Dacks decided he had moved a few inches towards the door, so he took the last but one throwing knife out of the cabinet as a precaution. It would give him pleasure, he thought, and looked more hopefully at the prostrate, repulsive figure on its back.

The first shot from upstairs was followed by an answering second and an ugly cry from above their heads and a thump. The first shot had obviously convinced Diogo de Almeida.

A volley of shots exploded and again all eyes looked up at the ceiling, but Dacks's upward glance was a feint and the throwing knife buried itself just below Norman's spine as he tried to lurch up and open the cabin door. He was struck motionless, on his knees, left hand on the door knob. A pitiful whine came out of him and a pitiful hand came round and fluttered below his newly sprung tail. A second knife took him down into hell. No one moved.

A single shot and another thump. Diogo de Almeida rarely missed when he was coldly annoyed. Dacks allowed himself a smile and hoped that one of the two bodies upstairs on the deck had been part of his revenge for Yasani.

"You're losing your friends rapidly, Harold. Where do you go from here? We don't miss, you see, unlike you with your spear guns. Such a pity for you, but then they are difficult things to use accurately. To take you back to Rhodesia would have its problems, as police always want to know the whole story and that would jeopardise the potential of my mining friends. I think it is better that you meet the customs of Africa face to face and then the old law will have been fulfilled. For this once you will take the consequence of your hirelings' actions. Without you, Yasani would not be dead. You are the basic evil that caused his death, not the man who fired the gun. Stupidly, foolishly, he did as he was told and his time will come also if it has not already come up on the deck. Oh dear, and there dies another one. What a horrible scream. You will have a chance, Harold, but a chance, I'm afraid, that is not very good. You are going to be left on the island of Bagota all by yourself and Yasani's friends and relatives will be told. Your people killed Yasani, you see, Harold, and the hunt that you will be part of is the local custom of revenge. You could try and swim the twelve miles to the mainland with the sharks, or you could try to hide yourself. The choice will be yours. Ah, your crew have stopped firing. I wonder if they are lying down dead or standing up with their hands above their heads. No, my friends, don't try anything. If you do anything now you will definitely be dead in a few moments."

Dacks looked away from the two guards. Harold Ackit's eyes were swivelling around for a means of escape, but his Adam's apple was unable to get a fraction further away from the point of the steel that he could sense with a vicious certainty was so close to himself. Dacks visualised the action on the deck and then looked up at the ceiling and bellowed.

"Diogo, we're down here!"

The cabin door was kicked open violently and bounced back shut just as quickly off Norman's dead head. Diogo de Almeida had seen all he needed to in that fraction of a second. The door opened again but quietly this time, and, with his small revolver showing the way, Diogo de Almeida looked around the room, coughed gently to indicate his surprise, then moved further into the cabin.

15

WITH THE COMPLIMENTS OF SAFARIS LIMITED

"You know, Mr Dacks, I really must say that the holiday was quite splendid. Everything about it was just as Thomas and I used to enjoy and that beautiful island was so peaceful and gentle, and so far away from everything. The atmosphere was absolutely pure. Yes, that was what I really noticed about it and it gave me such a sense of comfort. If I wasn't going to South America next year, I'd say that I'd come again, but I always really believe in going forward. Good things should be remembered and not trampled on in a second attempt. And I like this airport too. Clean, high-ceilinged and lots of friendly atmosphere. Yes, you really thought of everything for the Dacks's tours and you and Korina were such lovely hosts. I hope she'll be well soon. Such a horrible accident. I never knew that coral could be so dangerous. Well, it just shows how careful one has to be these days. And thank you again for your farewell gifts. I shall have that big drum in my dining room, and you were right about it being so light and with the case you lent me to carry all the extra things, I'll only be a few pounds overweight. Not that I can say the same for myself, as I must have put on pounds and pounds. But then there's no pleasure without pain."

"Don't you worry, Mrs Hall, my London agent will collect the case from you so that it won't litter up your flat. I always thought it was such a waste of money for people when I started these tours. Most people had to buy an extra case for their trophies just for the one journey. As far as I'm concerned it's a bit of advertising with its inscription of *With the compliments of Safaris Limited*. And as you know, you're not the only one needing to borrow a case as both Mrs Mure and Miss Featherstone needed one too."

"Oh but I do feel so sorry for dear Anna. Poor girl, she's cried all morning and he is such a nice man. Of course, that first love is always the most painful and even if they don't see each other again, they'll never forget. They'll build lots of castles in the air about how life could have been if they'd been old enough and he had had a job with enough money. She'll turn round in a street in ten years' time when she sees a man who reminds her of him, and it will all come back. To each other at the moment they are perfect and with Herman staying in Rhodesia and her soon to be six thousand miles away it will remain like this. You and I know there are ups and downs as there were with me and Thomas, but their memories won't have any. It's wonderful how life gives us these little things for the future."

Mrs Hall returned to the last of her Rhodesian martinis with a wistful look on her wise face that showed she was looking back deep into her own past. Dacks watched her with pleasure and thought of all the safe, trusted things in life that were epitomised by an English woman of her age and bearing. He looked out of the airport cocktail bar, through the open doors onto the balcony, over the heads of Herman Small, Anna Featherstone and Francine Mure, and at the crystal blue sky above the runway and deeper bush. Harold Ackit was dead and he felt no emotion whatsoever.

Dacks chuckled to himself and one dark eyebrow rose a fraction as he remembered the ten minutes he'd been the subject of Korina's wrath in the Salisbury General Hospital. Korina had spared him no words and he was fortunate she hadn't been fit enough to get out of the bed and hit him with something hard. She had thrown a small glass from the bedside table, but she had still been too weak to be accurate and without him having to move, it had missed him by three feet and broken against the air conditioning unit. He had made a mental note to be more faithful in the future and then his mind had gone back to the well-bandaged Anna-Marie, who he'd left on the island in Diogo de Almeida's house, and he wasn't so sure he'd succeed. His guests thought that Harold Ackit was also in that house with a bad case of malaria, drenched in hot, feverish sweat, but Dacks knew better. The sweat was cold and eternal. The corpses onboard the motorboat had gone down with the ship and the three remaining members of the crew were possibly still rowing towards Beira with a reasonable chance of success. Dacks's warm promise to kill them quickly if they didn't leave Africa within a month assured him he'd heard the last of them.

He was pleased that Herman Small was staying behind. The job he'd found him on a tobacco farm would be the beginning of a new life for him. The future was there to be taken and not looked for in dead men's shoes.

Francine Mure caught his eye and he smiled encouragement in response to the wistful regret in her expression. There was always a man at the play or the party. She would be all right, he thought, and even if she hadn't succeeded in attaining her goal she'd had a good holiday.

The Tannoy crackled and he looked up at the speaker above his head with a frown of expectancy.

"South African Airways announce the departure of their Boeing 727, Flight SA 276 for Johannesburg. Will all passengers take leave of their friends and proceed along the red route through emigration to the aircraft."

Dacks swallowed the last of his Lion lager, the drink he reserved for lunchtime drinking in airport bars, and visualised the three cases snugly secure in the belly of the three-engined aircraft. From Johannesburg, his friends would take another flight bound for London.

Anna Featherstone and Herman Small followed Francine Mure through from the balcony. Dacks smiled encouragement at the younger girl. They all went down in the lift and crossed the flagged space to the red route. Herman Small cared nothing for the stares as he kissed Anna violently. Anna reciprocated, then broke into tears and ran down the passage without a wave. Francine Mure followed after a handshake she hoped would end in a kiss but didn't. Mrs Hall followed and Dacks momentarily retained some of the warmth from her hand.

"Let's go up on the balcony," Dacks suggested to a silent Herman Small, "and wave them into the aircraft."

Herman brightened and followed him back into the lift, through the bar and out on to the long balcony. Half an hour later, the three other guests were smaller people down below as they walked across the tarmac to the tail of the Boeing with its belly dropped down into stairs. Anna turned and waved and so did the others.

Herman felt better and waved a strong return.

"It's a good country," said Dacks. "You're going to like it."

There was a smile on his face.

CAST OF CHARACTERS

Anna Featherstone — A naïve nineteen-year-old English girl
Anna-Marie — Bunny girl on Santa Salina island
Dinga — Waiter at the hotel in Mana Pools
Diogo de Almeida — Portuguese hotel owner on Santa Salina island
Francine Mure — A thirty-year-old wealthy divorcee
Gabe Saunders — Captain of the *Cara Mia*
Harold Ackit — A middle aged English banker
Herman Small — A young Englishman looking for adventure
Jimmy van Niekerk — BSAP Police officer and school friend of Mark
Joseph — A barman at the Casino Hotel in Victoria Falls
Korina Prague — Mark Dacks's assistant and co-host at Safaris Limited
Mark Dacks — The suave owner of Safaris Limited and principal character
Mnzedi — Friend of Joseph's father
Mrs Hall — A rich elderly widow
Norman — An acquaintance of Harold Ackit's
Sergeant Mzingwa — Member of the special branch of the BSAP
Yasani — Gabe Saunders's number two

DEAR READER

Reviews are the most powerful tools in our kitty when it comes to getting attention for Peter's books. This is where you can come in, as by providing an honest review you will help bring them to the attention of other readers.

If you enjoyed reading *In the Beginning of the Night*, and have five minutes to spare, we would really appreciate a review (it can be as short as you like). Your help in spreading the word and keeping Peter's work alive is gratefully received. Please post your review on the retailer site where you purchased this book.

Thank you so much.
Heather Stretch (Peter's daughter)

ACKNOWLEDGEMENTS

Our grateful thanks go to our *VIP First Readers* for reading *In the Beginning of the Night* prior to its official launch date. They have been fabulous in picking up errors and typos helping us to ensure that your own reading experience of *In the Beginning of the Night* has been the best possible. Their time and commitment is particularly appreciated.

Daphne Rieck (Australia)
Agnes Mihalyfy (United Kingdom)
Hilary Jenkins (South Africa)

Thank you.
Kamba Publishing

Printed in Great Britain
by Amazon

76623334R00099